Mafia-run towns are quiet— no one steps out of line

Nothing much ever happened in San Valdesto. The townsfolk were peaceful and law-abiding—even if some of them were retired Mafia dons.

No one wanted to know about a protection racket that terrorized the area's shopkeepers. No one tried to disband the local string of teenage call girls. No one worried about the drug dealers who kept the town's schoolchildren happy.
No one cared.

No one except Maude Marner—she cared a lot. But she got killed for her caring.

_"I made the mistake of opening
The Bad Samaritan and read until midnight.
Believe me, it's a pleasure to read a
real mystery again. I couldn't put it down."_
—Dorothy B. Hughes

Keeping you in suspense is our business

RAVEN HOUSE takes pride in having
its name added to the select
list of prestigious publishers
that have brought—in the
nearly one and one-half centuries
since the appearance of the
first detective story—the finest
examples of this exciting
literary form to millions of readers
around the world.

Edgar Allan Poe's
The Murders in the Rue Morgue
started it all in 1841.
We at RAVEN HOUSE are proud
to continue the tradition.

Raven House Mysteries

Let us keep you in suspense.

THE BAD SAMARITAN

William Campbell Gault

A RAVEN HOUSE MYSTERY FROM
WORLDWIDE

TORONTO•LONDON•NEW YORK•SYDNEY

For Irene Kaprelian

———————◆◆◆———————

Raven House edition published January 1982

Second printing January 1982

ISBN 0-373-63018-2

Copyright © 1982 by William Campbell Gault.
Philippine copyright 1982. Australian copyright 1982.

Printed in Canada

1

LOOKING BACK ON IT now, if Homer hadn't died I wouldn't have been able to move up here to San Valdesto and live a life of boring ease. Then again, if Homer hadn't died I never would have met Maude Marner, an old biddy who could qualify as my favorite person in snug little, smug little San Valdesto.

Homer was my richest uncle. He had become my uncle by marrying my richest aunt. Homer had earned his money; my Aunt Sheila had accumulated her fortune by never marrying a poor husband. Homer was her fourth. He had brought Aunt Sheila to an economic level where she could afford to stop thinking about money.

So she divorced old Texas-bred Homer and married a younger man who could introduce her to the arts and the finer things of life—which included her money.

Homer sat around in that dank castle she had made him buy in Beverly Hills, sulking and drinking. Homer could always handle booze; it must have been the sulking that flipped him.

I had my last look at Homer and my first look at his new Ferrari on a drizzly afternoon in March. I didn't know it at the time, but it was the Ferrari that was going to permit me to move to San Valdesto and become bored.

I was staring moodily out the window of my little pine-paneled office in Beverly Hills on a drizzly afternoon in March, under the letters that read: Brock Callahan—Discreet Investigation at Moderate Rates. My rates were still moderate, but my investigations covered some areas now to which the words "discreet investigation" might not apply. Substitute "muscle."

Looking down at the street below, I saw this smooth machine pull into the parking space below the window. I hoped that some sleek young thing would now step out of it and head directly for my office. I love to fantasize about the upper classes, especially if they're young and feminine.

But Homer stepped out of it, two hundred and forty pounds of Texas flab. He saw me watching him and signaled for me to come down to the street, which I did.

"How do you like it?" he asked me.

"It's beautiful. When did you get it?"

"Ordered it last week, got it this morning. Almost four and a half liters under that hood. Big engine, huh?"

"Four and a half liters," I said, "reads out to roughly two hundred and seventy-five cubic inches. My Mustang has two hundred and eighty-nine."

"Mustang?" He stared at me. "You must be crazy! I could buy half a dozen Mustangs for what that beauty cost me. That is a twelve-cylinder car, Brock."

"And worth every dime they stuck you for it. Homer, I'm happy to see you have rejoined the living."

"I'm going to try," he said. "God damn that Sheila!"

I said nothing.

His face softened. "I'm sorry. I apologize. I keep forgetting that you're her nephew."

"She is what she is," I said, "as we all are, male and female. But I always thought you were too much man to be ruined by a hundred-and-twenty-two-pound woman."

"I love her, Brock. God damn her! I loved her and I still love her and she ran off with that young puke. I ain't got too many years left, man!"

"You're sixty. I'll tell you the deal I'm willing to make you. I'll trade you my age for your money."

"No, you wouldn't. You don't know what I've gone through. It has been one stinking year!"

All over the world, I thought, even among the poor. "Maybe," I said, "you should take a trip back to Texas and show your old neighbors this new Ferrari. A dose of nostalgia might bring you back to normal."

He shook his head. "There's nothing there for me. Of course, I've got only you and Jan here. Those friends of Sheila's dropped me the day she left me."

"No loss, from what I've seen of them."

"You are so right! But this is a big town. There must be some live wires I can mix with. I mean, with a heap like this, a young chick might overlook a few wrinkles."

"Don't do it," I advised him. "Find some firm-bodied woman around forty-seven who can appreciate money and a virile husband. In the long run she'll make you a lot happier."

"I had one of those," he said.

Sheila, he meant. She was fifty-one, a month from being fifty-two, but only Aunt Sheila and I knew that.

He sighed and shook his head. "We must both be nuts, standing here in the rain and talking about girls. I'll see you later, Brock. When it clears up we'll play some golf, right?"

"Right," I said.

"I've got to get over to Poole's and buy me a beret," he explained. "I'll phone you."

Homer Gallup in a Ferrari, talking liters and wearing a beret. He was a long way from Texas and Texas thinking.

My dearly beloved, my Jan, was out of town, redoing Glenys Christopher's house in Montevista, San Valdesto's swankiest suburb. This was the third time Glenys had redone her Montevista home. Evidently there were no interior decorators up there she trusted like my Jan. I had met Jan at Glenys's house too many years ago. Glenys had lived in Beverly Hills then, in a house the Christophers had occupied for almost a hundred years.

I was lonely, but I didn't want any ready young thing, nor even a Ferrari—at the moment. What I wanted was a tall glass of Einlicher. Only Heinie had it, within walking distance. I alerted my answering service and walked over to Heinie's.

The Rams' season was over, the Dodgers' season hadn't started. All Heinie wanted to talk about was the Lakers, and I am not a basketball fan. So I sat on a bar stool and drank my beer and listened to all the things Heinie could tell me about the Lakers that I didn't want to know. While I listened, the drizzle turned into rain, and the rain turned into a downpour.

Around six o'clock, I asked, "Do you have anybody in the kitchen who can fry a steak? I'm hungry."

"Of course I got somebody in the kitchen! I got dinner trade. What do you think this is, a dump?"

"A joint," I corrected him. "I've had a greasy pan-fried steak here for lunch, but I didn't know big-city dinner eaters liked that kind of food."

"You're not the only gourmet in town. What kind of steak were you considering?"

"Anything that didn't come off a horse. Whatever your best is, I'll have that."

So I had a juicy, greasy filet while his dinner crowd poured in, four men and two women. When the Laker pregame show came on from Seattle, Heinie had no talk for me; his eyes were glued to the tube.

I went home to my little Westwood pad through the slashing rain, through the glaring headlights of Wilshire Boulevard. The unmarried newlyweds in the next apartment were discussing her parents tonight. Their arguments were always louder and longer when her parents were under the adolescent microscope. Some loud and unidentifiable wailing was blasting from the expensive hi-fi of the U.C.L.A. students on the other side of me. The noise died after a while and the angry words from the other side reverted to giggles. Peace and quiet descended on the smoggy village of Westwood.

I slept. I dreamed. In Green Bay, the snow came down and Vilas ran straight at Horse Malone, my flanking partner on defense. You can run around Horse with a minimum of effort and speed. There is *no* way you can run over him.

But Vilas had never been short on ego. Horse hit him above the hips, and put the top of his helmet into Vilas's chin. The ball dropped to the frozen ground, and bounced high.

It bounced right up into my waiting hands and away I went, my only moment of glory in all those years with the Rams, my only touchdown.

The dream was interrupted this time. I was two yards short of the goal line when the referee's whistle blew—and blew and blew. . . .

It wasn't a whistle, it was my phone ringing. I was back in my lumpy bed. It was three o'clock in the morning, and my phone was ringing.

The voice on the other end was soft and unctuous. "Mr. Callahan? Mr. Brock Callahan?"

"Yes."

"Sorry to disturb you at this hour, sir, but the police have insisted on identification and—"

"Who is this," I interrupted, "and who's dead?"

"I'm calling for the Westwood Village Mortuary," he said. "There was an accident out near Malibu earlier tonight and a man tentatively identified as Homer Gallup—"

"I'll be right over," I said.

It was only two blocks from my apartment and the rain had stopped. I walked over. The big double front door of the place was locked; there was a small night-light over the side entrance to the parking lot.

The door opened as I approached it. A tall, thin man in mortuary black was silhouetted against the dim light from the hall behind him. "Mr. Callahan?" he asked.

"Yes."

"I'm George Ulver. This way, please."

He led me down the dim hallway to a door, and paused. "He, uh, went through the windshield. I hope—"

"I'm sure I've seen worse," I said.

The room was cold. The body was on what looked like an operating table. There had been some rearrangement of the facial features, but I nodded. "It's Homer Gallup," I said.

"Would you come to my office, please?" he asked. "There are a few papers—"

I should have been sad. I should have been sick, after looking at that disfigured face. But my dominant thought was—that damned fool!

In the narrow office, I asked, "Why here? Why isn't he at the morgue?"

"The police phoned his home," Ulver explained, "but evidently he lived alone, without servants. Mr. Gallup belonged to the Los Angeles Funeral Society and his membership card was in his wallet. We handle the funeral arrangements for the society's members."

"It's all arranged, then?"

He nodded. "Mr. Gallup filled out his instruction forms six months ago and we have a copy. He wished to be cremated and his ashes sent to a mortuary in Texas. I'm sure they have his instructions there, but we'll check it, of course. Now, about relatives...?"

"The only one he ever mentioned to me was a cousin in Houston. I can't think of his name right now, but I'm sure I can get it for you."

Ulver checked through the papers on his desk. "Abner Shaw?"

"That's the man." I took a deep breath. "Was anybody else involved in the accident?"

He shook his head. "He was alone. He hit a bridge abutment at what the police called an extremely excessive rate of speed. The alcoholic reading in his blood was—"

"High," I finished for him. "It has been, ever since I've known him. Where are those papers I have to sign?"

When I went out again, the drizzle had resumed. There would be no funeral, not even a memorial service, so there was no point in phoning Jan now. He had spelled it all out on his instruction sheet. Though he had lived high, he would be cremated for less than two hundred dollars. Why not? Homer didn't like to pay for parties he didn't enjoy.

As for my Aunt Sheila, she was honeymooning with her new conquest somewhere in the Virgin

Islands, a strange place to take *her*. If Jan wanted to notify her, she could. My affection for Aunt Sheila was at its all-time low this damp morning in Westwood.

When I phoned Jan, later that morning, Glenys answered the phone. "Brock? Are you coming up for the weekend?"

"I hadn't planned to. Could I speak with Jan? I have bad news."

Jan's reaction was the same as mine. "That damned fool!" she said.

"I suppose there's no point in trying to get in touch with Aunt Sheila. She wouldn't be interested. When are you coming home?"

"As soon as that furniture gets up here from Beverly Hills. When is the funeral?"

"There won't be any. His ashes are probably on the way to Texas by now."

"Why don't you come here? You could play golf with Skip Lund."

"Not on those crummy public courses he plays. Sandpiper is the only one worth playing, and it's jammed on weekends."

"For your information, snob, Skip no longer plays on the public courses. He is a member of Pine Valley Country Club."

"Skip? When did he get that kind of money?"

"I suppose he got it the day he married June Christopher. You remember June, don't you—June Christopher, Glenys's sister?"

"Vaguely. Okay, I have a credit check to take care of tomorrow, but maybe Saturday. I'll phone you."

Skip Lund had married money. At Stanford, Skip and I had played in two Rose Bowl games, I as a humble lineman, he as one in an impressive succession of Stanford quarterbacks. Our graduating class had voted him the only one most likely to succeed.

He hadn't succeeded in the pros, and had gone up to San Valdesto after two bad years in the pay-for-play leagues. There, he bought a small filling station in the Mexican district and earned just about enough for beans and franks.

Three years ago he had become involved in trouble with the law, and loyal Brock Callahan had gone up there (at no charge) to clear him—and make myself no longer welcome, at least to the police, in that perpetual vacationland ninety miles from here.

Now he had fulfilled his classmates' prophecy; he had succeeded the easy way. Now, maybe, I would get partial payment for a full week of investigative work I had squandered on him. Pine Valley Country Club in Montevista was one sweet golf course.

I could use some clean air and a weekend among the idle rich. Jan is a decorator and all her clients are rich. That is probably the main reason we had never got married.

So, on Saturday I packed my swimming trunks and my golf clubs in the old Ford and drove up to San Valdesto, a town with a minimum of smog and a maximum of rich people, a retreat from reality.

The opponents Skip lined up for two days of best-ball competition were rich enough to make their bets scarey to me, but not to them. Or, I suppose, to Skip now.

I've forgotten the name of one of them; he was a friend of June Christopher's, a visitor from Carmel who had sharpened his skills at Pebble Beach.

The other player wasn't easy to forget; he was a real tiger, who carried his partner on both days. His name was Silas Marner. He had explained to

me on the first tee on the first day that he had
been named after his mother's favorite story.

I think that was the last word he said to me until
we were drinking in the clubhouse later. Between
the first tee and the eighteenth green, Silas
Marner insulated himself from all the amenities
and concentrated on winning.

After the showers and over the booze, he became a human being again. After the second
drink, he invited us all over for dinner the next
night.

2

THE MARNER HOME was probably expensive, designed by a famous Swedish architect, a strangely angled tall and wide structure, featuring California redwood inside and out. It was in Slope Ranch, a suburb on the other end of town from Montevista.

To my middle-class, pedestrian taste, it looked a little outré. But the food was great, the company genial, the liquor free. The man, I decided, who threw those kinds of parties could be forgiven both for this house and for his "winning is everything" conduct on the links.

It was a buffet dinner, and we weren't the only guests; there must have been at least twenty. The dialogue decibels rose as the alcohol went down.

I was seeking a quiet corner when Si's mother beckoned to me from the doorway to the den. When I went over, she said, "It's quieter in here, and I'd like to talk with you."

Either Silas Marner was a great reader or a compulsive book buyer; three of the four walls in the room were lined with books.

Mrs. Marner was a woman of about sixty-five, thin and short. Her gray hair was pulled straight back, her simple yellow linen dress could have been expensive, but I didn't think so. Her bright blue eyes in that thin, tanned face seemed to sparkle in the room's dim light.

"Si told me you're a private investigator," she said.

I nodded.

"Have you done any missing persons work down there in Los Angeles?"

"Some," I said. "Let's sit down. That noise was getting to me out there."

"And me," she said. "Yakety-yakety-yak. And nobody says anything. I can't understand how Si can stand it. He's not nearly as dumb as he looks." We sat together on a leather couch.

"Judging by his library," I said, "he can't be very dumb."

"Oh, not that way. But when he isn't playing golf or reading, he's throwing parties. Is that a constructive life?"

"I guess not, ma'am."

"Don't call me ma'am. I'm not *that* old. My name is Maude."

"Okay, Maude. Who is this missing person, a lover?"

"Watch your tongue, Callahan. It's a girl. I'm not sure she's down in Los Angeles, but that's the last place her friends up here know about. She stopped writing to them some time ago."

"Do her parents live up here?"

"Yes. Her mother is a waitress and her father is a slob. It's the mother I worry about. She's a good friend of mine."

"Has she made any effort to find her daughter?"

"None."

"Then why—"

"Never mind the why. I want to find her. You could send the information to me and the bill to Si. I don't live with him here. I live down where the people live."

"I knew we were soul mates," I said. "There won't be any bill. You give me your address and her name and I'll prowl around when I'm not working on a case. Okay?"

"Okay." She handed me a slip of paper. "It's all right there. Now, go and join your drunken playmates."

"I'd rather sit here with you," I said.

"I don't blame you. So run out and get me a glass of sherry and yourself another tumbler of booze, and we'll talk about something besides golf and bridge and capital gains."

I brought her the sherry and myself another jolt, and we sat in that book-lined room and talked about other things. Si was her only child, I learned. His father had died when he was twelve, and that's when she had begun to work. Si had started as a carpenter's helper when he finished high school, and wound up as one of the state's biggest builders, a real Horatio Alger story.

"I can't understand a man who worked that hard winding up with these—these butterflies!" she said.

"It couldn't have been all work with him. Nobody who plays six-handicap golf could have spent all his time working."

"He started caddying when he was ten, during the school vacations," she explained. "He was always tall and he lied about his age."

"The habit persisted, he's no six-handicapper. I've played against scratch players with weaker games than his."

"He is a very competitive man. I suppose golf is the only outlet he has for it now."

Then, from the doorway, my beloved said, "What are you two party poopers doing in here?"

"Getting away from a poopy party," said

Maude. "When are you going to marry this wonderful man, Jan?"

"When he decides to get into some sensible work. Brock, if you're going home tonight, we'd better leave. It's almost midnight."

"Okay. I'll be in touch with you, Maude."

"Thank you. Jan, you'd better grab this man while you can."

An hour later, Jan stood next to my waiting Mustang and asked, "Why can't we get married and live up here?"

"What could I do up here?"

"I have about seventy thousand put away. You could buy some kind of business with that. You're not dumb, Brock."

"And I'm not Skip Lund. I earn my own way, lady."

"Oh, for heaven's sake! Seventy thousand dollars hardly ranks me with the Christophers. Call it a loan."

"Dump me," I said. "There must be a dozen solid citizens you could marry in this town. You really don't need me. I need you, but you don't need me."

"No more than my heart," she said. "Damn you! Get the hell out of here! Go!"

"When will I see you?"

"When I come over the horizon. Good night!"

I kissed her and headed for home, back toward Westwood, back to reality.

Skip was sure living high off the hog, the worst thing that could have happened to him. At university he had been considered a great passing quarterback, but Stanford had turned out other quarterbacks who, though with far less natural talent than Skip, had gone on to fame, fortune and glory in the pros. In the pay-for-play leagues, *everybody* on the squad puts out two hundred per-. cent, or you can forget about the Super Bowl. Skip had been born too good; it had made him less than he should have been.

He had never had to work that hard in college, not learned to work that hard when it paid off. He had his skill and his charm and his looks. It had been easy for him to marry money. He could have done it a half dozen times when he was at Stanford.

I had thought that crummy little gas station he ran in San Valdesto would finally make a man of him. When you are making a living selling an independent brand of cut-rate gasoline in competition with the major oil companies, man, you are putting out. Those big firms take a dim view of free enterprise. Skip had survived. Given time, he might have been successful.

I cut over to the coast road at Oxnard, to get away from the jammed freeway traffic—and spent an extra hour in the going-home traffic from the beaches.

I had no job scheduled for tomorrow; maybe I could prowl Sunset and then the Venice district and ask my contacts there if they had ever run into a girl named Patty Serano.

She could be living the free will, free speech, health food life in Venice or the life of a hooker on Sunset Boulevard. With today's kids, there was no way of knowing.

Nor, as I settled into my lumpy bed, did I have any way of knowing that I, too, would be starting a new life tomorrow.

3

THE NAME of the law firm was Weede, Robbins, McCulloch and Adler. The woman who phoned me next morning was Grant Robbins's secretary. Could he see me at two o'clock this afternoon?

Business on Friday and now a new job to start the week. Things were picking up. "I'll be there," I promised.

They were a prestige firm and would pay my top rates. It probably wouldn't be divorce work. If it was, I'd take it. Earlier in my career I wouldn't accept divorce work. Earlier in my career I didn't handle bail bonds, either. Hunger and the advancing years can alter adolescent attitudes.

His office was spacious and paneled, with a couple of Degas pastels on one wall and a Matisse print on another. He was a tall man, well tailored and quiet voiced.

He shook my hand and said, "You don't remember me, do you?"

I smiled, admitting nothing.

"You nailed me for an eighteen-yard loss," he prompted, "when you were at Stanford."

I remembered him now, a sub quarterback for Cal. "I remember," I said. "You almost beat us before the afternoon was over."

"My best day," he admitted. "We never had a winning day against Stanford when you and Lund were there. But who did? Sit down, Brock, and prepare for the news. Unless you've already heard it?"

I shook my head and sat down. This didn't sound like divorce work.

"We represent the estate of Homer Gallup," he started—and my mind went blank.

Maybe I suspected. I don't know. I didn't hear anything for almost a minute.

Then his voice broke through. "Are you all right? You're pale. What's wrong?"

"Nothing serious. Start over from where you told me to sit down. I missed most of the rest of it."

In nonlegal terms, Homer's cousin in Houston and Brock Callahan of Westwood-Beverly Hills were the only heirs to the estate of Homer Gallup. Our shares would be equal.

It was a vulgar thing to ask, but I'm vulgar. "How much?" I asked.

He shrugged. "It's almost impossible to estimate, with estate taxes what they are these days. It should be substantial."

"More than twelve dollars?"

He smiled comfortingly. "At the most conservative estimate, you can be assured; once we're through probate, that you'll be able to live very well without diminishing the principal."

I didn't go back to the office. I went directly to Heinie's for a shot of bourbon and a beaker of Einlicher. Then I phoned San Valdesto from Heinie's wall phone.

Jan was there. I told her. "You always wanted me to amount to something and I finally have."

"You landed that insurance company retainer," she guessed.

"I don't need it. I have inherited half of Homer's money."

A silence on the line.

"Jan?"

The silence continued.

"Jan, are you there?"

"Have you been drinking?" she asked quietly.

"I had an ounce and a half of whiskey and one tall beaker of beer—*after* I got the news."

"You got the news from a man in a bar?"

"I got the news from a partner in the most distinguished law firm in town, Grant Robbins of Weede, Robbins, McCulloch and Adler. They're handling the estate. We can be married now, Jan. When?"

"Tomorrow, if it's true. You stay in the office this afternoon and you stay home tonight!"

"I'm picking up my golf clubs and coming up there," I told her. "To hell with the office!"

"Brock, are you *sure*?"

"Once we're through probate, I'll be solvent. Until then, we'll skimp along on your little seventy grand. Tell Glenys to lay an extra plate for dinner."

"I'll be waiting," she said.

I still had another duty to perform before I left town. I drove over to Wilshire and down to the impressive offices of the Calvin National Investigative Service.

They had offices in every major city in the country, and they handled all the kinds of investigative work anyone would never need. Lately they had been doing a lot of missing persons searches. The daughters of the rich had turned into wanderers and the fathers of these girls wouldn't be likely to hire any cheap peeper for that delicate a mission.

I've forgotten the name of the local manager, a gray man. Gray hair, gray complexion, dark gray suit.

"Brock Callahan?" he said, and I thought he sniffed. "Aren't you a—a private investigator?"

"Yes. But I have to go out of town for a while, and I've a case I was supposed to start on today. I thought, perhaps, as a professional courtesy, you boys could work on it."

"Professional courtesy? Our rates, Mr. Callahan, are based on our rather expensive overhead. Is your client prepared to pay our rates?"

"I doubt it. But I am. This is more than just business, the woman who hired me is a good friend."

"I see. You realize we require a retainer."

"I do. Unfortunately, at the moment I am rather low on funds. I could give you a couple hundred. And if you wanted to check my credit, you could phone Grant Robbins, of Weede, Robbins—"

He held up a hand. "I know the firm. You've done work for them?"

"At the moment," I said, in my most refined voice, "they are working for me. They're handling an estate in which I am a major beneficiary."

"One moment, please." He got up and left the room. When he came back to sit behind his desk again, he asked, "Is this a local case?"

"It's a girl who is missing," I said. "She lives in San Valdesto but the last knowledge of her whereabouts was in Los Angeles."

His phone buzzed. He picked it up and said, "Yes. I see. Thank you."

He smiled at me. "There will be no need for a retainer, Mr. Callahan. If you'll just give us what facts you have? It's a runaway case, I presume?"

"More or less." I gave him what facts I had, including Maude Marner's address. I said, "I appreciate your trusting me."

He didn't even blush. He smiled and said, "Professional courtesy."

JAN AND I were married by a Unitarian minister in the formal garden of the Christopher acreage in Montevista a week later. A week after that, she found a little cottage in the same general area that she was just aching to redo, a little cottage of three bedrooms, den and three and a half baths. Because it was what is known in the real-estate trade as a "fixer-upper," we were able to buy this gem for two hundred and eighteen thousand dollars.

Hard work, honest dealing, persistence, intelligence—and being Aunt Sheila's nephew had finally earned me the financial security that is every American's birthright.

I had always been told by my seniors that retirement can be boring, and I learned some new truths in the next couple of months. Golf should not be played seven days a week, unless you're inclined to masochism. There are actually men with I.Q.'s over seventy who play gin rummy. There are otherwise rational people who think bridge is a serious game.

On the personal level I learned that raising my voice and drinking more didn't make life any less dull.

"You're bored," Jan said, one morning at breakfast.

I had shared many breakfasts with Jan over the years. The moral novelty of having her sit there as a wife was still new. I nodded.

"You miss padding around in the smog, playing the Junior G-man," she went on in a way she has. "You can't get conditioned to success."

"Success? An accident of birth, a chance marriage and then an inheritance—is that the road to success?"

"Many of the people we have met here inherited their money," she explained patiently. "They're not as unhappy as you seem to be."

"Maybe they're dumber. They're certainly dull enough."

"Because they aren't always arguing or getting stoned?"

"Let's not fight," I said. "Why don't we drive up to Solvang today and window-shop and eat some Danish food?"

"I'd love that. But Julie Marner is expecting me for bridge this afternoon and it's too late for her to find a substitute. We'll do it, though. Tomorrow, I promise."

Julie's husband, Six-Handicap Si, was over at the club, looking for a game when I got there.

"If you're willing to play for small stakes," I told him. "I know when I'm overmatched."

"I'll tell you what," he offered. "We'll play for the same stakes and I'll give you one more stroke on each side."

That was the way we did it; that was the way I lost. The man was a natural gambler, a legitimate tiger. If he needed a thirty-foot putt, he made it. If a two-footer didn't matter, he missed it. I shot my best round ever on the course and he took me all three ways on the Calcutta, plus four presses.

At the nineteenth hole he reverted to his off-course decency and bought me a beer. I had decided to forgo the hard stuff for at least one day.

"How's your mother?" I asked him.

"I can't be sure," he said. "She's become very secretive lately. She mentioned you this morning when I phoned her." He shook his head. "She wanted to know if you were still a working detective."

"Tell her I'm a nonworking bum."

He frowned. "It can't be that girl again, that one she was looking for a couple months ago?"

"I doubt it. The best agency in the country spent

two weeks on that and came up with nothing. What do you think she's onto? Some shenanigans?"

He stared at me blankly.

"You said she's become secretive," I explained. "She's looking for a detective. Put those two facts together, Dr. Watson, and what do you come up with?"

"My nosy mother," he answered. "I've told her a thousand times to keep her nose out of other people's business. What did it ever get her?"

"What's the medal the Chicanos in town give their most admired citizen?"

"The Good Samaritan medal."

"That's what it got her. Ever get one, Si?"

"Jesus," he said, "a moral private eye. There's a dichotomy for you."

"For you, not for me. Of all the people I've met in this town, including you, she's number one. As a matter of fact, she's the only one I've met."

"Only what?"

"The only citizen," I said.

He laughed. "Jan warned me about you. Brock the Rock, the righteous Ram."

"I wish somebody had warned me that you were here today. I would have left my money at home. You tell your ma if she needs me, I'm available. Tell her it's free—if you can pronounce the word."

"You sure lose hard. How about tomorrow? I can arrange for transportation if you need it?"

"Find another sucker. I'm going up to Solvang with my bride."

"What's in Solvang?"

"Danish beer. Thanks for the game, Si."

"Thanks for the money. I'll tell my mother you're still available."

Jan was home when I got there. She had won

almost three dollars at bridge, she informed me proudly. She had been a dollar and twelve cents in the red and then made a grand slam, doubled and vulnerable.

I put my hand on the wall for support. I stared at her in trembling disbelief. "You're lying! Nobody has ever done that!"

She looked at me coolly.

"A joke," I explained.

"With a touch of rancor," she added. "You're not happy, are you?"

I thought about that for a second or two, and decided, "I'm happier than I was in Los Angeles. I think my trouble is, I'm not as happy as I expected to be. Let's go out for dinner, just the two of us."

"Okay. But let's talk about you, first. Maybe it's not working that bothers you. You've always had this middle-class hang-up about the evil idle rich, haven't you?"

"I guess. Don't fret about me. I'll think of something productive to do, eventually. Matter of fact, Si told me today Maude's been suggesting she might need a detective."

"Oh? You like her, don't you?"

"Very much. A real down-to-earth woman. Maybe we ought to phone her and ask her if she wants to go up to Solvang with us tomorrow? She loves that Santa Ynez Valley."

"Some other time. I think we ought to be alone for one day."

I didn't press it. I should have, and maybe. . . . Maybe, hell: I have enough sins of omission on my conscience without adding one postfact guilt about an omission as innocent as that one.

We didn't go to a fancy restaurant. There was a pizza parlor in town that served Einlicher. We ate there, piling up the calories, loving every bite.

And then a good night in the hay. It was Shaw who said it, I think: the nicest thing about marriage is that it combines the ultimate in temptation with the ultimate in opportunity.

THE UPPER-CLASS CITIZENS of the Santa Ynez Valley didn't play golf and drink and play bridge. They rode horses and drank and played bridge. The more photogenic inhabitants stood around horse shows in elegant clothes, affording newspaper photographers glossy groupings for the Sunday society pages.

But their country was pastoral and peaceful, soothing the nerves, quieting the doubts. And the shops of Solvang offered the imported china, silver and fabrics that stirred the refined love of beauty in my bride, and triggered her vulgar acquisitiveness.

We came back down the San Marcos pass considerably poorer but happier, Jan with a deck full of gewgaws, me with a belly full of Danish beer. The lights of our town were spread out below us all the way to the sea.

"It's not a bad town," Jan said. "Too much happened to us too soon. We got—disoriented."

"It's a great town," I said. "Now that we're friends again, who was it that doubled you when you made the grand slam, vulnerable?"

"Julie Marner. She's very competitive."

"So is her husband. Nobody is perfect, Jan." That was the beer talking.

"People don't have to be perfect. But they could have some compassion and some awareness and a rational sense of values and an open mind."

"Wouldn't that be wonderful?" the beer said. "Then they'd be just like us!"

4

THERE WAS NO local morning paper in our town, and the *Los Angeles Times* had gone to press too early to cover the story. We got the news of Maude Marner's death on the local radio while we were eating breakfast the next morning.

She had been discovered by an occupant of the trailer court where she lived, slumped in the front seat of her Volkswagen, a victim of carbon monoxide.

There had been a long vacuum cleaner hose stretching from the tail pipe through the stuffed vent of a front window. The engine was still running when she had been found. The noise of the engine, at three in the morning, had finally disturbed her sleeping neighbor and he had gone out to investigate. According to the police, she had apparently been a suicide.

Not Maude Marner. No way!

Jan stared at me. "Yesterday, you suggested she— Maybe, if we had invited her to go along...?"

"No!" I said harshly. "Don't say it, don't think it."

"We might have talked her out of it, Brock."

"Out of what? Jesus, you don't believe that bilge about suicide, do you? Maude Marner?"

"The police—" she started to say.

"I have met the police in this town," I reminded. "Skip Lund would still be in jail if we had relied on the police in this town."

She said nothing.

"What do we do?" I asked her. "If we phoned the Marners, I wouldn't know what the hell to say."

"Don't phone now. There's nothing you can say now. But murder, Brock? With the neighbors as close as they must be down there, could she be killed that way? How long could the engine run before neighbors became suspicious?"

"I don't know. I plan to run down to Kelly's Kourt this morning to find out."

"Do it," she said.

Kelly's Kourt started with the mobile homes fronting on Rivera Street and seemed to go on forever, down a long driveway to the trailers, to the half dozen or so remnants of the original, ancient tourist cabins at the far end.

The complexions darkened along the route. I passed through the pasty-whites of the mobile homes, through the light brown of the trailers, and almost to the coal-black inhabitants of the age-old leaning cabins. It was an integrated neighborhood, poor, poorer, poorest.

Maude Marner's residence was among the cheaper trailers, and glaringly out of sequence: a forty-foot aluminum Hashua. She probably needed the room; she had housed many an adolescent runaway.

There was a police car parked in front of it. A uniformed officer was talking with a man I recognized—Detective Sergeant Bernard Vogel.

This was the officer who had tried to railroad Skip. At least, that had been my possibly prejudiced view of him. The feeling I had then, and still harbored, was that Sergeant Vogel was a stubborn champion of the upper dog, a toady for the powerful.

He recognized me as I got out of my car, and muttered under his breath to the uniformed man. When I came closer he said, "Callahan, isn't it? I read in the paper that you had moved up here, in the society pages. Marry money, peeper?"

"Don't flex your muscles, Sergeant," I said. "I'm here because Maude Marner was a friend of mine. I hope you aren't the officer who came up with that silly suicide theory?"

"It's Lieutenant Vogel now," he said stiffly.

"Congratulations!"

He glared at me. The uniformed man glared at me. When you've been glared at by N.F.L. linemen, all cops look like midgets, but I was not here to rekindle old grudges.

"Could we start over?" I suggested. "I'm a local citizen now, and Maude Marner was a woman I admired very much."

"Name me somebody who didn't. Okay, we'll start over. Anybody hire you for this?"

"Nobody. I'm retired, Lieutenant. I played golf with her son the day before yesterday and he more or less told me his mother was onto something. I heard the news of her death on the radio an hour ago."

"Silas Marner told you his mother was onto something? What's that supposed to mean?"

"He told me she had become secretive lately. And she had asked him if I was still a working detective. So I put two and two together, and guessed she had to be investigating some shenanigans, somewhere."

"Maybe she had learned something about her son, or maybe somebody got to her because of him. Did you think of that?"

"I'm not following you, Lieutenant."

"Silas Marner," he said, "got his big start in the construction business in Vegas and around La Costa. That's where he made most of his money. Now, if the syndicate hoodlums had a reason to want to scare him—"

"You're reaching, Lieutenant. I think you just went over the cliff. Marner worked for the legitimate hotel chains in Vegas."

"Sure. You opened the line, not me. We had it pegged as suicide." He told the uniformed man, "Take that stuff back to Sergeant Helms. Tell the chief that I'll be in for the conference at two o'clock."

The uniformed man nodded, took one last malignant look at me and went away.

Vogel took a deep breath. "Now that you're an establishment figure, Callahan, you don't have to hate cops anymore."

"I never did. Only the bad ones."

He stared at me. "Was that personal?"

"In no way. I think, when we worked on opposite sides of that mess Skip Lund got into, we didn't part as friends, but we had developed more respect for each other."

He shrugged.

"Be fair, Lieutenant. You had something personal against Lund."

"Maybe. I've lived in this town all my life and seen a lot of poor but handsome gents find rich wives to keep them from working. Lund hadn't married money then, but he sure was hanging around with the girls who had it."

"I wish Skip would go back to work. He worked like hell at that crummy station he was running. For your information, I didn't marry money. I inherited it. We're on the same side of the law now, Lieutenant. Should we start over?"

His smile was thin, but it was a smile. He held out his hand. "Okay. Now that you're rich."

I shook his hand and asked, "What did you send back to the station?"

"Some letters and stuff. Every minority organization in town and the American Civil Liberties Union have been on our necks since seven o'clock this morning. You can tell your friend Marner that this case is going to get the full treatment."

"I'm sure he knows that. But I don't report to him and I'm not working for him. Could I go inside?"

"If you don't touch anything. It has been gone over very thoroughly by experts."

"I know. I just wanted to see how she lived. I've never been to her house, though we've been friends since before I moved up here. I just want to take a look. Like all establishment figures, I'm sentimental."

A touch of her fragrance still lingered—yellow laundry soap. She used it to wash her hair, she had informed me, to give it sheen. The place was immaculate and standard, everything built-in, everything designed for twentieth-century compact living.

Some of her many awards were framed on the wood-grained metal walls; even the most humble servant in the service of the Lord is not above displaying his (or her) symbols of achievement.

Vogel had come in with me. "I'll probably wind up in one of these. Not you, huh?"

"With taxes what they are, who knows? What were those papers you gave the uniformed officer? Was she writing a book?"

"Nothing like that. Mostly letters."

"And who is Helms? Your lab man?"

He gave me the cool-cop look once more. "Being a concerned citizen doesn't entitle you to a badge.

Why don't you join the other concerned citizens who are meeting with Chief Harris at two o'clock?''

"Thanks for the invitation. Lieutenant, I read the local paper. I read how you boys are always moaning about being understaffed and underpaid. Here I am, trained, muscular, perceptive—and free! Why all the friction?''

"I remember your tongue," he said. "And I've got a sour bias on private eyes. I've seen enough of their shoddy work.''

"Not of mine. Though I admit I could have gone that route. I was about one step away from it when my uncle died. And I swear to you I have no angle in this case.''

He shrugged. "I'm not the boss. Talk it over with Chief Harris. I'll go in with you. You can meet Helms there, too. He's not our lab man. He's Maude Marner's favorite cop. Seen enough here?''

"For now. Sterile, isn't it? Not my kind of living.''

He laughed. "It sure as hell ain't Montevista!''

I talked with Sergeant Joe Helms in his small office while Vogel went in to inform his boss of my presence.

Sergeant Helms was a mahogany-hued man, wide, thick and uniformed. He was Mexican, Puerto Rican and probably some black, he explained to me.

"And some Anglo, the Helms," I guessed.

He nodded. "My paternal grandfather. Twenty years ago I would have come in here as a janitor. But today, with all the racial tension—'' he shrugged ''—call me the minority public-relations man.''

"You worked with Maude?''

"At times. And with the Urban League and the

A.C.L.U. and half a dozen other outfits in town. The new police image, you know—"

"You sound cynical, Sergeant."

"Frustration can make a man cynical. This is a real stingy town when it comes to anything that smells like welfare."

"I know. I've listened to some of our leading citizens orate on the subject. You don't think Maude committed suicide, do you?"

"Who can know? According to her doctor she had some kind of cancer. Nobody here released that story. I don't know where the media got it. I would guess, if Maude Marner decided to take the big step, she would have found a more ladylike way, maybe sleeping pills."

"Autopsy finished?"

He nodded.

"Anything? Pills?"

"Nothing but carbon monoxide."

"What about those papers Lieutenant Vogel sent in? Have you looked them over?"

His smile was slight and scornful. "Letters. I have no idea why he sent them in. Don't quote me, but Bernie Vogel . . . ." He shrugged. "Well, if I don't say anything you can't quote me. If you're going to be working on this, you can look at 'em."

"I'm not sure I'm going to. Chief Harris and I didn't exactly make music the last time we met."

"I heard about that. You were an L.A. peeper then. Now you live in Montevista. To Chief Harris and Lieutenant Vogel, that could make a big difference. That is another nonquote, you understand?"

I nodded.

"If you work on it," he continued, "you'll probably be working with me. I am their minority star on this one."

"We're both big enough," I said. "I hope we're bright enough."

Vogel came in a few seconds later to tell me that the chief would see me now.

He hadn't changed much, penguin shaped, snow-white hair, red face. His voice had lost some grate, but it still jangled the nerves. He stood up from behind his desk. "Well, Mr. Callahan, we meet again!" He held out a hand and managed a smile.

"It's been a while," I said genially.

"Hasn't it, though? The Avila business, wasn't it?"

"Lund," I corrected him. "Warren Temple Lund, known as Skip."

"Of course, of course! Sorry. Lieutenant Vogel tells me you would like to act as a sort of citizen observer on the unfortunate affair of last night."

"I had hoped for a more active role than observer, sir."

"Yes, of course. That was—badly phrased. Dealing with the public, as I have to, I have developed a tendency toward euphemisms. But that's neither here nor there. Lieutenant Vogel thought you could work with Sergeant Helms. The lieutenant will work with both of you for a day or two."

"Then you plan a longer investigation, than a day or two?"

His soft face hardened. "I plan to stay with it until no citizen in this town has any grounds for complaint."

I nodded.

A trace of softness returned to his face. "There will be a conference in this office at two o'clock this afternoon. Some of the bleeding hearts—I mean, some of the leaders of various citizen groups will be here. I thought we might suggest you as their representative on the investigation. Weren't you with the Dodgers, or the Lakers?"

"The Rams, sir. That was some time ago."

"Well, very few of 'em are young. They'll probably remember you. At two, then?"

"I'll be here. Thank you, Chief."

I went out into the corridor and saw a ghost talking to Vogel. I couldn't remember for a few seconds where I had seen him before. And then, as I walked over to join them, I remembered the tall, thin man silhouetted against the hall light that gloomy night.

"George Ulver," I said, "of the Westwood Village Mortuary."

He nodded, frowning.

"I identified Homer Gallup's body at your place this spring," I reminded him.

He nodded again, his face showing no recognition, and turned back to Vogel. "The way it is, with Mrs. Marner, you see, she belonged to the local South Coast Memorial Society and we handle all the funeral arrangements for the society's members. I was wondering just how soon we—"

I went down to the fountain for a drink of water while Vogel explained to Ulver what forms were required before the department could release the body.

When he had finished, he asked me, "Ready for lunch? Maybe we should talk about that two-o'clock meeting?"

"Let's go to the club," I suggested. "I'll buy."

"Montevista?"

"Pine Valley."

"That's kind of fancy. I'd better wash first."

"You can wash there," I said. "We installed running water last week."

We took my car. He stared at it before he got into it. "How old is this heap?"

"Fifteen years. It's the first year Ford brought 'em out. It's a classic, man."

"Sure. I guess if you're rich enough, you can drive anything."

In the grill at the club, another ghost was at the bar when we entered. At least, it was a ghost for Vogel, or maybe an ogre.

Skip Lund saw me, started over, saw Vogel—and stopped.

"Keep coming, Skip," I said. "That was a long time ago and we're all grown up now. Come on over and shake Lieutenant Vogel's hand."

"Sorry!" Skip said curtly. He turned back to the bar.

"Maybe I don't blame him," Vogel commented quietly. "He's not the only local citizen who thought I tried to railroad him. How come they let him into a fancy club like this?"

"He's a fancy guy," I said, "just like I am. All Stanford grads are fancy guys."

"That translates into rich."

"Maybe. When you tried to railroad him, he was a poor guy. You can't win 'em all, Bernie."

"I can't win any," he said. "My poor wife has to work as a part-time school librarian."

5

Jan was on the phone when I got home that afternoon, complaining to the Beverly Hills furniture store again about another late shipment.

When she hung up, she said, "Glenys wants a new sofa and she insists I order it through them. It's frustrating!"

Jan and Sergeant Helms, they both had their frustrations, though in separate worlds. I smiled at her.

"Well?" she asked.

"I think I'll go back to golf and booze. I might even try that gin rummy. I spent an hour and a half this afternoon in a room full of social activists. If these are the only people concerned about the people, the people are in trouble. But maybe they deserve to be, if you follow me."

"I'm trying to. Are you saying you've become a misanthrope?"

"I'm a Pisces, and you know it. I think I'll have a drink."

"Would it be your first today?"

"It will be my third. I had two at lunch with an officer by the name of Lieutenant Bernard Vogel."

"Make me one, too," she said. "And then we'll sit here peacefully and you can tell me about your day."

We sat in the peaceful room and I told her about

my day. On the road in front, the cars went by, the Mercedes, the Porsches, the Cads and the Continentals, even a couple of Rolls-Royces. The working rich were going home to their martinis.

All those fancy people rode past our tiny quarter-of-a-million-dollar cottage in the fringe area, while I recounted my day.

When I'd finished, she said, "Sergeant Helms sounds nice. Isn't Lieutenant Vogel the man who tried to jail Skip?"

"The same man. He was a sergeant then."

"I still don't understand about the conference in Chief Harris's office. What was the point of it?"

"The department was getting a lot of static about Maude's death being called a suicide. To be chief you have to be more than a cop. It's a political job."

"It might have been suicide. Maude had cancer, you know. Couldn't the chief simply issue a statement?"

"Not to social activists. They demand an encounter. They prefer a small room, so their screams can bounce off the walls. Harris handled it with real political savvy. He maneuvered them into screaming at each other—and then turned the meeting over to Vogel."

"And the letters?"

"Nothing, so far as I can tell. I brought home Xerox copies. I think I'll have another drink."

"You don't need it. You're having Einlicher with dinner. I made some enchiladas. I want to get you conditioned for Fiesta. That's next week, you know."

Fiesta Week in San Valdesto. Nostalgic people trying to recreate a synthetic past. I could hardly wait.

MAUDE MARNER IS DEAD. That's real enough. Concentrate on that, misanthrope. The sun went down, the night came on. The enchiladas fought with the Einlicher, causing rumbles in my stomach.

I had learned one thing from the letters: Maude had bridged the generation gap. That square old girl, full of corn-pone homilies, had reached the unreachable kids. The letters were from Laguna, Toronto and Monterey, Taos, Sausalito and Amsterdam, all havens for youthful wanderers.

Their parents' homilies had driven these wanderers away from home; how was Maude different? To define her in her own language, she practiced what she preached.

These kids, to use the phrase of another homily master, Mr. Ernest Hemingway, had their own sensitive, built-in shit-detectors.

I voiced this thought to Vogel as we stood in front of Maude's mansion next morning.

He nodded. "They trusted her. We trusted her. She turned a few of them in, if they were likely to become dangerous."

"She get along with all the cops?"

"I can't name you one who didn't like her."

"But there must have been some kids who didn't, the ones she turned in. Anything there?"

"Not so far. We'll be working on it."

"Another thought I had last night, that engine running so long and nobody coming out to investigate. And then I realized, if I lived here, I wouldn't come out at night to investigate any strange noises."

"One man did. Let's go over and talk with him. He works from four o'clock to midnight. He should be home."

Home was a twenty-two-foot trailer across the street. An enormous American flag flew proudly from a mast on top of it. The occupant was American, too, standard American red-neck in a T-shirt, beefy and belligerent, a man named Al Pilot.

"That motor wasn't running more than ten minutes," he told us from his doorway. "That was horseshit what you read in the papers, as usual. It didn't wake me. I was watching the late-late show."

"You were the only neighbor it bothered?" I asked him.

"I was the only one with guts enough to come out. I'm prepared, see? I got me a twelve-gauge pump in here and a .30-.30 and a big Colt .45 semi-automatic." He paused, to look down the street. "You live around some kinds of people, you better be armed."

I must have shown some reaction; he smiled knowingly. "You got me figured for a bigot, right, muscles?"

"I expected it," I said, "when I saw the flag on your roof."

"What the hell's that supposed to mean?"

"Nothing I could explain to you in the time we have. We're here for answers, not to give lectures. You were the only one who came out and she was in the seat next to the driver's seat?"

"That's right."

"Safety belt buckled, shoulder harness, the whole bit?"

"Right! If you guys are thinking murder, look for one of them greasy longhairs she was always feeding." He gestured toward the ancient leaning cabins at the far end of the street, the dark-complected end. "Or one of *them*."

Vogel said evenly and coldly, "Just answer the questions, we'll handle the investigation. What time did you get home?"

"I told two cops already. About one o'clock. I stopped at Ordano's for some groceries. They're open all night."

"Her car wasn't there at one o'clock?"

"Like I told the others—no. Anything else?"

Vogel sighed, shook his head and looked at me. "Brock?"

"No, no questions."

"Don't forget what the cops say on the late-late show," Vogel said. "Don't leave town, Mr. Pilot."

He sneered—and clanged the metal door shut.

Vogel expelled a long breath.

"This case is looking less like suicide every minute, isn't it?" I said.

"Why? You figure somebody drove her around town in her car with that hose sticking out the window and back to the tail pipe? I suppose he was wearing a gas mask? Nobody would notice anything that strange driving around town?"

I said nothing.

"Motive, means and opportunity," he reminded me.

"I know. Otherwise, it's manslaughter—or suicide?"

"You're half-right. Suicide needs the same three. Let's go and talk to the manager."

She was a thin, fairly young woman with a washed-out look and bleached coarse hair. The darkest thing on her was the discoloration around one eye.

"My loving hubby," she explained before we asked. "He drinks. Next question?"

"We're trying to establish what time Mrs. Marner left here yesterday."

"All I know is what I told the last cop who asked. Her car was there around five o'clock, when my old man came home. When we went out for a couple of beers, around seven, it wasn't there. Didn't nobody down there see her leave?''

"They were probably eating at that time," Bernie said. "Between five and seven, there aren't many people outside, are there?''

"There's always enough," she said, "night and day. I guess, outside of Mr. Pilot, they just don't notice what's going on around 'em.''

"And he was at work?''

She nodded. "He drives past here five afternoons a week at exactly three-forty-five. You can set your watch by that man. And you don't have to wait for his rent money, either.''

"You and your husband own this court?''

She stared. She snorted. "Us? You gotta be kidding. A dump like this? Immigrants and outsiders, they own the dumps like this in San Valdesto. We're native Americans, mister.''

Bernie nodded wearily. I said, "Let's go, Lieutenant. I want to look at that empty lot next door.''

We went over to the lot through a heavy silence. I said, "She should have warned us. She should have put Old Glory on her roof.''

"Right. And taken the time to learn some history—and grammar.''

We stood knee-high in grass and weeds littered with discarded beer cans, looking over at the backs of all the trailers on Maude's side of the court.

He said, "You were thinking the engine could run here for a while? You were thinking that ten minutes of carbon monoxide from a Volkswagen tail pipe isn't a long enough time?''

"I'm not sure what I was thinking. It was dumb, I realize now. But that street over there—'' I pointed toward the slanting street that fronted this triangle lot ''—a man could park there. He could gimmick Maude's car to make it look like suicide, and then walk back across this lot to his own car, and—''

"You're going too fast for me," he said.

"Carbon monoxide is carbon monoxide," I said. "She didn't have to be gassed in her own car. If it was suicide, why the safety belt? Does that make sense to you?"

"Nothing in this case makes sense to me. Who would want to kill a saint?"

I looked at him doubtfully.

"Dumb," he admitted. "They have a very high mortality rate, don't they?"

"The highest. Pilot heard her car running. Maybe it was there but not running when he came home. Did anybody ask him that? We didn't."

"Let's check the record at the station," he said. "I don't want to look at that son of a bitch twice in one day."

We drove through the authentic small-town ghetto of Rivera Street and turned right on Main Street, into the fraudulent neo-Spanish of small-town commercial America. White plaster and red tile, with a touch of imitation adobe here and there.

New shopping centers had sprouted on the edge of town, so the downtown merchants had narrowed Main Street to afford more sidewalk room for the strolling window-shoppers, and multiplied the parking lots.

"My father had a kosher delicatessen here twenty years ago," Vogel said. "He wanted me to take it over. I was too snooty for that. A college man running a delicatessen?"

I said nothing.

He said, "We get smart when it's too late, don't we?"

"Some late, some never. Why the department?"

"Don't ask me. Maybe I wanted to bounce around some of the goyish bully boys who bounced me around when I was a kid. That's a hell of a reason to be a cop, isn't it?"

"Better than some I've heard. You could have done worse."

"I could have had a rich uncle, too. Check in with Helms, if he's back. I'll see what we have in the records on Pilot."

6

THE DEPARTMENT'S mahogany-hued minority public-relations man, Sergeant Joe Helms, was in his small office talking on the phone. The ashtray on his desk was overflowing with cigarette butts, the odor of stale smoke was heavy.

He hung up and said, "A waitress I know, a woman named Mary Serano. She might have something for us."

"Does she have a daughter named Patty?"

He nodded. "Why?"

"Maude was looking for her a couple of months ago. She must have been doing it for Patty's mother."

"Want to come along and talk with her?"

"I'll ask Bernie if he needs me first."

Vogel had some paperwork to do; I went with Helms.

"This Mary Serano," he briefed me, "is a waitress in a little Italian restaurant Maude liked." He chuckled. "And she drives a Cadillac."

"Does she answer calls in her free time?"

"Not Mary. She's got a big, jealous husband. She books. Small bets at first, half-dollar horseplayers. She must have banked her pennies; she'll handle anything up to a century note now."

"You never busted her?"

"Now and then, just to keep her humble. Who gets hurt? Everybody gambles."

"You don't think somebody a lot bigger might be banking her?"

He shook his head. "I keep an eye on her. Even Maude would blow a dollar with her once in a while."

"Maude Marner bet on the ponies?"

"If the odds were right. Her son is probably the third-best poker player in town." He paused. "After Vogel and Paul Pontius."

"Who's Paul Pontius?"

"A guy who lives out your way...a rich guy. He's retired now."

"What did he do before he retired? That name seems to ring a bell in my mind."

"I can't answer the bell for you. I have my own ideas, which I am keeping to myself."

"Vogel plays rich man's poker?"

"About once a year, when Si Marner or Pontius invite him to fill in. Mostly he plays in cheaper games with his friends. Vogel, I think, likes to mix with the upper classes. He can be rough on the peasant types."

"Most small-town cops are."

"Not me, mister. I'm as peasant as a man can get."

The waitress who booked horses, Mary Serano, lived in a pleasant house on a solid middle-class street, undoubtedly the only waitress on the block. She was about fifty, but without sag or wrinkle.

When Helms introduced me to her, at her door, she asked, "Are you the Callahan who is a private investigator in Los Angeles?"

"I was."

"Mrs. Marner sure thought a lot of you." She held the door open wider. "Come in."

In her well-furnished living room, she told us,

"Maude was in for dinner a couple nights ago. I mentioned to her about this man who threatened me. That happened the night before. I went out to my car, in that lot near the alley, and this man was waiting for me. He told me if I didn't close down shop, I'd wind up in a wheelchair."

"How come you didn't tell me about this when it happened?" Helms asked.

"I didn't know the police protected bookies from each other. And besides, I have plenty of friends with muscle."

"But not with guns. You could be way over your head, Mary."

"I'll take my chances. Anyway, when I told Mrs. Marner about it, she seemed real disturbed. She said she was going to look into it."

Helms smiled. "If I had a dime for everything she told me to look into, I'd be retired. Where would she start looking?"

"Who knows? If it's connected with gambling, her son could know. He sure plays in some big money games."

"But not with hoodlums."

"Huh! You mean when they get rich enough they're no longer hoodlums?"

"Get off that kick, Mary. What did this guy in the parking lot look like?"

"I couldn't tell in the dark. He was short and he was skinny. I saw what he was driving, though—a yellow El Dorado."

"He doesn't shape up as a small-timer," Helms said. "You were planning to retire, anyway, weren't you?"

"I didn't plan to be scared into it."

"You could cool it for a while, couldn't you, while I check around?"

She shrugged.

I asked, "Was that the last time you saw Mrs. Marner?"

She nodded.

"How was her mood that night?"

"Cheerful, same as always. But if she had troubles, how would we know? Other people's troubles bothered her more than her own."

On the way back to the station, I asked, "How come you let Mary operate? Is that standard department procedure?"

He smiled. "We go a little easier on the locals we trust. In the no-victim vices only, you understand. Rough stuff gets rougher treatment."

"She's an informer?"

"No way! Just a local free enterprise bookie."

"And how come you do detective work in uniform?"

"I explained that to you yesterday. Image, man! The cop with heart, the minority citizen's fuzz, the longhair's friendly pig, all in one visible package, wrapped in department blue."

I spent the afternoon at the station, up to my navel in papers—interrogations, dossiers, rumors, reports and records, the dismal history of society's losers, the men without rich uncles. Vogel had called it right; Maude's death was getting the full treatment.

A thought nagged at me as I gathered up my notes, a picture that couldn't come into focus. It went away as quickly as it had come. There was nothing in these papers that revealed even one of the deadly triplicate the courts demand: motive, means and opportunity.

Was it possible that Maude had committed suicide? Means and opportunity she had. But no motive had come to light in an afternoon of reading.

I went home at four o'clock to an empty house. I hadn't had a drink all day. What better time than now, free from the disapproving eye of my spouse? I poured four ounces of distilled corn into a tumbler, added ice, and took it with my notes into the den.

The whiskey was consumed, the tumbler washed and put away, a bottle of Einlicher half-gone, when Jan's little Mercedes chattered into our driveway.

"Anything new?" she asked.

"Two astounding revelations. Kelly's Kourt is no longer owned by a man named Kelly and Si Marner could be the third-best poker player in town."

She looked at me suspiciously. "A liquid lunch again?"

"Two Big Macs with fries and cole slaw." I counter-attacked. "Where have *you* been?"

"With Julie Marner, all afternoon. She's coming around. But Si is still in a daze. They're dropping in after dinner."

I said nothing.

"I'm going to have a drink," she said. "Should I bring you one?"

"I'll stick with the Einlicher. Bring me another bottle."

When she came back, she said, "Si was touched when I told him about your interest. But honey, if it's going to depress you—"

I thought of what Raymond Chandler had written: "Down these mean streets a man must go. . . ."

I said, "Being depressed by the poor isn't much worse than being bored by the rich."

She started to say something, evidently changed her mind, and sat down next to me on the couch. "Where did you hear that about Si?"

"From a cop. Did we ever meet a man named Paul Pontius?"

"You should remember him. You got into a very loud argument with him at the Marners' house one night."

"Was he a fat man, with gray hair, a big man? A 49er fan, wasn't he?"

She nodded. "And you were drunk. I guess he was, too. I'm glad to see you're back to beer. You handle that better, Brock."

I tried to remember the evening, but it was hazy. I said, "Do you think you could find out where the Marners met Pontius?"

"I am an interior decorator," she said, "not a detective. I don't spy on *my* friends."

I didn't rise to the bait. I said with quiet dignity, "Okay, then I'll do the dirty work that has to be done. I'll ask him tonight."

She went to the kitchen to prepare our dinner, as a noninvolved citizen should. I sat there nursing my beer, as the name of Paul Pontius rolled around and around in my weary brain. I had seen that name in print; I hadn't remembered it from the party. But where?

Si's wife, Julie, was sweet enough when sober. She was a shade on the chunky side, but a sexually attractive woman. She was a cheerful birdbrain before her third drink, a lachrymose one thereafter.

"You're a wonderful person, Brock!" she greeted me. "You are a true friend!"

"Thank you," I said.

"Anything new?" Si asked. "Have those Keystone Kops downtown come up with anything?"

"Nothing yet. Neither have I. Where do we start?"

"I have no idea. Is Vogel working on it? He's one of the few bright ones down there."

"I've been working with him and Sergeant Helms."

"That could be the cream." He slumped into one of our matching barrel chairs. Julie took the other.

Jan and I sat on the couch. There was nothing to say and nobody said it for a few seconds. Then Jan asked, "Drink?"

Julie nodded. "I think we should. Bourbon and ice, please, Brock?" Si wanted Scotch, Jan a weak bourbon and water.

I made the drinks and poured myself a cup of leftover dinner coffee. I handed them around and sat down next to Jan again. There was still nothing I could think of to say.

Si took a paper from his pocket. "There are some names here, mostly kids. Some she helped, some she turned in to the law. There might be some I've forgotten; I'm still checking. That last name, he's a lawyer she worked with from time to time, one of those A.C.L.U. do-gooders."

I took the list. I wanted to ask about Pontius, but how? He was only a name that troubled me. Mentioning him now might seem to connect him with the murder.

I took a side road. "Vogel's a good cop, you think?"

He shrugged. "Don't you? I don't know about police work. I played poker with Bernie a couple of times and he struck me as a very sharp operator."

"Last case I had in this town," I explained, "he and I didn't get along. We do now, and I think he's sharp, as you said." I took a sip of coffee. "How can he play your kind of poker on his pay?"

"He doesn't play it often. When one of the regulars doesn't show up, Paul calls him for a fill-in."

"By Paul, do you mean Paul Pontius?"

"That's the man. You and he almost came to blows at our house."

"Oh, him? As I remember the evening, he was a

very arrogant guy. And also stoned that night.''

"The pot," Si said, "has just described the kettle. And he's as big as you are, too. Don't mess with him, Brock.''

"I'll be careful. Where did you meet this oversized kettle?''

"At Vegas. He had some lots on the Strip I was dickering for.''

"How did Vogel happen to meet him? Through you?''

"I think they knew each other before that. They probably met at some poker game somewhere.'' He stared at his Scotch and then looked up to frown at me. "You really led me down that road, didn't you? You're thinking Paul Pontius could be a hoodlum front and Bernie Vogel might be involved with him?''

I shook my head.

There was some rasp in Si's voice. "I've mingled with a few hoodlums, working where I did. We both know I'm not what San Valdestans refer to as 'old money.' Most of the people we know, we wouldn't know if Julie hadn't gone to school with Glenys Christopher.''

"Si, please—'' Julie said.

I said, "I wouldn't know *any* of them if Jan hadn't decorated the Christopher home here and in Beverly Hills. I'm not getting your point, Si.''

"Maybe I don't have any. Maybe all I have is resentment. My ma brought me up with this old-fashioned idea that real men earned their own way.''

I smiled and stood up. "You need another drink, tiger. I think we're both off our natural terrain. We should have stayed on the other side of the tracks.''

"Men!'' Julie said. "Do you understand men, Jan?''

"Rarely," Jan said. "I think maybe it's time for all of us to have another drink."

"The same?" I asked.

They all nodded.

"Si," I said, "you read me wrong. Pontius interests me, but I wasn't trying to tie him up with Vogel."

"Okay," he said. "I was out of line and I apologize. Why should Pontius interest you? Because of the squabble you had with him?"

"Probably. I'll make the drinks."

The evening was strained after that. Jan was just waiting for them to leave so she could tell me off. Julie chattered on, trying to brighten the general mood. She achieved her goal finally—by leaving before her third drink.

When the door closed behind them, Jan said, "You're more devious than I realized."

"Only professionally."

"In your devious way," she pointed out, "you were cross-examining one of our friends. Wouldn't you call that bad manners?"

"I'm not an expert on the subject of manners," I told her. "I'm inclined to Maude's philosophy; I'm more concerned with conduct. And there is one important fact we must not overlook, social butterfly. Maude Marner is dead. That is the only important fact I'm concerned with now."

7

I HAD NEVER HAD a high opinion of lawyers, but Stanley Nowicki looked closer to a human being than most of the breed, a thin, intense young man with warm brown eyes.

In his storefront office on lower Main Street, I said, "Si Marner gave me your name as an attorney who worked with his mother from time to time."

"I worked with Maude," he admitted. "I'm surprised that her son would give you my name—he never approved of her working with me."

I smiled. "I know. He called you one of those A.C.L.U. do-gooders."

"How about you? Is do-gooder an obscene phrase to you, too?"

I shook my head. "I phoned you because I thought you might have something that would help me with—with what happened. I have a closer affinity with you boys than Si has. As you too often do, I'm working on this case without compensation."

It was his turn to smile. "In the interests of justice?"

"Probably not. Call it. . . ." I shrugged.

"Being a citizen?" he suggested. "I've been thinking of all I knew about Maude since you phoned. I've been checking her connections and interests—and come up with nothing. Could you call back this afternoon? I'm due in court in half an hour."

"Okay." I looked around his office. "I suppose you don't get much carriage trade here?"

He smiled again. "We don't refuse it. Were you contemplating a substantial retainer?"

"A donation," I said. I sat at his desk and wrote him a check.

He stared at it. "A thousand dollars? This could make you a lifetime member of A.C.L.U."

"No, thanks," I said. "You use it where it will do the most good. I'm not a joiner."

"Neither was Maude," he said sadly. "Thank you very much."

I went out with banners flying, with the sound of distant trumpets in my ears, out into the sunny morning on lower Main Street, the Mexican end of it, studded with minority-owned restaurants and Anglo-owned loan offices.

Up this mean street I walked to the next corner, turned left toward Aqua Street and there found an eating place less likely to be infested with cockroaches.

I consumed two Egg McMuffins there with two cups of coffee and the *Los Angeles Times.* Our new coach had been hired, I read. He would bring the Rams back to glory. There was still hope for civilized man.

The stockbrokers had been working for hours, even the fat-cat lawyers were probably driving to their offices, when I arrived at headquarters.

Vogel wasn't there. I showed the list Si had given me to Joe Helms. He kept nodding as his eyes scanned the names, then looked up and said, "I know most of them. I'm not sure these addresses are current. These kids move around a lot."

"You think they're worth checking out?"

. He snorted. "With a case as crazy as this one, who knows?"

"Want to go along, or do I work with Vogel today?"

"Vogel's got to go to court this morning. And I'm going to try to smoke out that punk who scared Mary Serano. Why don't you take it alone? If you get any kickback on your authority, tell them to phone us here."

The first name on the list was Danning Villwock. He wasn't one of Maude's kids on either side of the ledger. He was a retired probation officer she had worked with while he was still active.

I couldn't call him to arrange a meeting; he had no phone. I drove up into the hills, the gray, tinderbox late-summer hills, along a narrow winding road, climbing all the way.

The rutted road that led in from his mailbox was worse, designed for vehicles with four-wheel drive. My groaning steed almost made it. I walked the last two hundred yards to a cabin built of railroad ties, shaded by a grove of eucalypti.

There was a jeep in the side yard. In the small front yard, a man of about fifty in knee-length cutoff jeans and no shirt lounged in a deck chair with a can of beer in one hand, dreaming out at his impressive view.

He got up as I approached. "Morning, stranger."

"Good morning. Are you Mr. Villwock?"

He nodded, frowning. "I've met you somewhere. Or seen you."

"My name is Brock Callahan."

"Hell, yes! That Lund business. Didn't I read somewhere that you live in town now?"

"Since April. Si Marner gave me your name."

He nodded. "Maude's boy. You working on that?"

I heard you'd retired when you got all that money.''

"Charity work," I explained. "Some view you've got."

"Today," he admitted, "you can see the islands. You can see it all today."

The city stretched out below, seventy thousand bugs in a snug rug. Beyond it was the sea, and the Channel Islands. You could see our famous Mission from here and our more famous courthouse and the state university buildings of the U.C.S.V. campus. You could see all the gray, dry hills around us, waiting for one careless match.

"Maude used to sit here with me," he said quietly, "and smoke a little pot and complain about the state of the world."

"Maude Marner? Pot?"

He nodded. "I doubt if she smoked it in front of her runaway kids. I smoke it only when things get sticky. Want some?"

"No, thanks. I have enough bad habits now. Wasn't that kind of phony of Maude, telling the kids one thing while she did another?"

"I don't make those kind of judgments," he said. "We all have our masks. If it was a flaw in Maude, it was a flaw she shared with most of those kids' parents."

"But Maude, with her Puritan ethic—"

"I repeat, I don't make judgments. Want a beer?"

"I thought you'd never ask," I said.

We all have our masks. . . . I sat in the deck chair next to his while he went into the cabin, a tall, sinewy and apparently adjusted man. But we all have our masks.

He came back with four cans of Olympia in a rusty bucket of ice cubes. He handed me a can and took his seat again. "Who put out that suicide story down at headquarters?"

"It wasn't official. The uniformed officer who answered the call made some casual remark about it looking like suicide. It still does, technically. But not psychologically."

"And that's why you're here?"

I nodded.

He put the cold can of beer to his sweaty forehead. "She was up here two days before she died. Something big was troubling her this time, something bigger than runaway kids or mistreated Chicanos. Usually, when she had her long nose in somebody else's business, she confided in me. But not this time."

"Maybe she was having personal problems."

"Maybe. I was never a man for investigative police work. Parole and probation, that was my bag. When I worked with Maude, before I retired, it was usually about cutting down some kid's probation period. She was sharp about the ones we could save."

"You retired young," I said.

He smiled. "Is that an accusation? I was never on the take, if that's what you mean. I'm single and a man of simple tastes and I invested my pennies wisely. Is Vogel working with you?"

"For a couple days, according to the chief. Sergeant Helms will stick with it after that, I guess."

"Good combination. Vogel's got the brains and Helms knows the people. Helms grew up with the people he's now putting into the clink." He smiled. "Or else he's lecturing to them. The new cop image, that's our Sergeant Helms."

I said nothing.

"Getting along all right with Vogel?" he asked. "You two tangled once, didn't you?"

"We did. I get along with him now. I get the feeling Helms doesn't like him much."

"A lot of the boys down there don't. Vogel can read without moving his lips and some cops are suspicious of that. And they might wonder about him playing poker with Pontius."

"Paul Pontius? Why does that name seem famous to me?"

"You don't remember? The L.A. *Times* gave it half a page when the story broke. They do love to put the rap on anything that happens in Miami."

Miami, that was the trigger word. "I remember now," I said. "It was that real-estate investment trust the S.E.C. was investigating, and the Justice Department, too. A Mafia front outfit, wasn't it? They bilked a lot of rich men out of some big money."

"Right. And who came down from San Francisco to defend them? What big-shot attorney got all seven of them off scot-free?"

"Paul Pontius."

He nodded and took a deep breath. "There are some things I could tell you about this town, but maybe I'd better keep my big mouth shut."

"Whatever you tell me will stay with me," I said. "I'm not a cop, and I can keep a secret. And maybe what you tell me will find us the bastard who killed your good friend Maude."

"Okay. Another beer?"

"I'm ready for it."

He tossed me a can. "That new condominium development out near the university, that's *all* mob front money. So is that new hotel down near the beach, and a number of apartment houses in town. You see, this is a retirement town. And all kinds of people retire here, including several mob big shots who are getting long in the tooth."

"Do you have some names?"

"Not at the moment. If your investigation leads you along that route, I might change my mind."

"The local police aren't worried about syndicate infiltration in this town?"

"It's not an infiltration, it's a residency. Look, these old Mafiosi didn't care how much blood ran in the gutters when they lived in Detroit or Chicago or Brooklyn or Newark. But they're *retired* here. This is their sanctuary. The dirty money they could pick up in this town is small change compared with what they're making in real estate."

He sipped his beer. "They know that. And they know if the small-time hoodlums here ever get organized, they might be retired in another Detroit or Newark. They don't want that. They've done the department a favor several times when I was working down there."

"They worked together, the department and the Mafia?"

"Never. That's a fairly honest department, Callahan. Better than most, I'd judge."

"So what was the favor?"

"If some bush-league hoodlum down there got too big for his britches and started to organize his brother hoodlums, he would suddenly be found dead. That happened twice while I was with the department."

"I suppose, to complete this cynical story, the department didn't give those cases any extra effort?"

"Would you? There are too many decent people getting killed and robbed and raped and assaulted. There are so many hours in a working day. What would your priority be?"

"I don't know. Is Si Marner one of the names you won't reveal?"

"Jesus. You're really reaching! How could he be involved in his mother's death?"

"Well, even Bernie thought maybe some mobster had a reason to scare Si, and this was his warning."

"Does he really? And still he plays poker with Marner—and Pontius?"

"I'll have to ask him about that. I'll tell him I remembered that piece I read about Pontius in the *Times*."

"Be damned sure you don't mention my name."

"I won't." I handed him the list of names Si had given me. "Could you look this over and pick out the worst apples?"

He scanned it. "Most of them look harmless to me. This Tishkin, now, Lenny Tishkin, he's a very sour apple. This Jesus Gonzales used to pal around with him, but Gonzales, according to what Maude told me, was starting to straighten out. Lenny is the worst of this bunch."

"Thanks a lot," I said. "I hope you're wrong about the Mafia. I'm not big enough to tangle with *them*."

"Who is?" he said. "Not even the Feds. Good hunting, Callahan."

I went down his rutted driveway to the winding road. Halfway down that, a punk in a Porsche came whining up impatiently behind me, riding my deck, crowding for a chance to pass, when any sane citizen would know there was no chance to pass on a road this dangerous.

I could have stopped, pulled him from his car and muscled him into a little respect for his fellow motorists. There was a time when I would have, before Homer died.

Today, I waited for the first chance to pull over onto the dry grass and let him zoom by. Today, I was sueable. Wealth has its disadvantages.

I rode on in my careful, solid-citizen way, heading for the domicile of Jesus Gonzales, on Vista Court.

Vista Court was a dead-end alley that opened off Rivera Street. The one-room, sink and toilet apartment of Jesus Gonzales was on the second floor, over a welding and brazing shop.

His wife was there. She had a baby on the floor and another in a crib and another in her arms. She couldn't have been more than twenty.

Jesus, she informed me sadly, had left her two weeks ago. He had bought himself the poor man's divorce, a bus ticket out of town. The only Jesus she had left was there on her wall on His cross.

I didn't bother her with questions. I went down the outside steps and out the alley to Rivera Street. About a half a block from where I stood was a place called Chickie's. Like Kelly's Kourt, it was no longer under the original management. Juanita Rico owned it. She made the tastiest enchiladas I had ever eaten.

There were only two customers in the high, dim room, one black, one Mexican. Juanita was behind the bar, jet haired and olive skinned, a hundred and forty-eight pounds of woman.

She recognized me instantly and that warm smile brightened the room. "I knew you'd be back someday. But you went and got married, you bastard! You knew I was single, and you went and got married!"

She had a macabre sense of humor. I had seen her make herself single in this very room by emptying both barrels of a twelve-gauge shotgun into her husband's stomach.

"I married the woman I loved, Juanita. It wasn't your body that brought me back. It was your enchiladas."

She sighed. "Some nasty tongue. And here I put in Einlicher, in memory of you." She pointed at the spigot.

"You've got Einlicher on draft? Hurry, hurry, hurry!"

She drew me a beaker and said, "I made some enchiladas this morning. We could eat together, couldn't we, at that little table in the corner, as we did so long ago?"

She was a very sentimental woman, away from her shotgun. I said, "I'm sure my wife wouldn't mind. Especially if I don't tell her."

The enchiladas went down to join the Egg McMuffins, the Einlicher was introduced to the Olympia. "You still book, I suppose," I said.

"I never did, and you know it. But if you've got a hot horse, I'll go dollar-dollar with you on him."

I remembered Joe Frisco's line, and used it. "Not so loud," I whispered, "we don't want to change the odds."

She laughed. "Smart-ass! And now you're rich. You must be something to live with!"

"Did you know Maude Marner, Juanita?"

"So that's why you're here. I knew her."

"You don't sound as if you liked her."

"She helped my people, a few who deserved it and a lot who didn't. I've never been on welfare. Nobody in my family has ever been on welfare. But, today we go on it with no shame at all."

"Mine, too," I told her. "Five hundred generals in the Pentagon, and almost every one of them started his welfare career at West Point when he was seventeen."

She shook her head. "You never did make much sense. No wonder you had to marry your money."

I said nothing.

"I apologize," she said softly.

"I wasn't sulking, I was disappointed. If anybody should be friends, I thought it would be you and Maude Marner."

"I liked her. She was a good, warmhearted woman. But sometimes people like her can do more harm than good. You're old enough now to know that."

"Let's not argue. Do you know Jesus Gonzales?"

She made a face. "A good example. Just takes off! Leaves his sweet wife and three wonderful babies and *adiós*!"

"I know." I took three hundred dollars from my wallet and laid the bills on the table. "Would you use this to buy her what you think she might need? Don't tell the welfare people. It's none of their damned business!"

"Yes, *amigo*. I hope, with your heart, that your wife is watching her money."

"That's enough of that," I told her coolly. "Our money is money *I* inherited. My wife was down to her last lousy seventy grand when I saved her."

She smiled. "I knew it! That Callahan, I told myself, would never marry money. He's too proud and too dumb." She laid a hand on mine. "Am I going to meet her? Are you going to bring her in here for my enchiladas?"

"We'll be in. But now I'm here for your help. Will you keep an ear open? There isn't much that happens down here that you don't hear about."

She nodded. "I'll be all ears and no mouth."

"You wouldn't happen to know a short, thin man who drives a yellow El Dorado, would you?"

"What's an El Dorado?"

"A Cadillac, a front-wheel-drive Cadillac."

She shook her head. She smiled. "What are you driving these days, Pancho?"

"A Ford, same as always."

"But not your wife, I'll bet. She has class, huh?"

"Too much, at times. A car is transportation, Juanita. I've outgrown status symbols."

"I always pictured you on a horse," she said. "A big white horse, strong enough to carry your armor. Go with God, *amigo*. The enchiladas were on the house."

8

It had been an expensive day so far, a thousand-dollar whim and a three-hundred-dollar lunch. And unproductive, except for what Villwock had told me—which I still only half believed. I went back to headquarters to compare notes with Helms.

Vogel was with him, helping him fill the ashtray. "I'm stuck in court for the afternoon," he told me. "I was scheduled to testify this morning, but that damned Nowicki is defending. That man could keep a parking ticket in litigation for two years."

"Stanley Nowicki?"

Vogel nodded. "One of those A.C.L.U. bleeding hearts. Do you know the man?"

"I talked with him for a few minutes this morning. Is he a bad lawyer?"

Helms chuckled. "Bad lawyer for Bernie. That makes him a good lawyer for his client. Did you come up with anything?"

I shook my head. "Nothing that would help us. I learned that Jesus Gonzales has deserted his wife and three children."

"It figures," Helms said. "Gutless Gonzales, one of Maude's lemons. She sure wasted a lot of her time on him."

"How about the man who threatened Mary Serano?"

"Nothing solid. There's a chance I might know more later today. Did you hit the whole list?"

"I hardly got started on it."

Helms grinned and patted the holster that held his .38. "I'll go with you this afternoon. Gotta protect our citizens against those hostile hippies."

He didn't go with me. I went with him, in a department car. The first two addresses were fruitless; the former occupants had moved on and left a rental deficit. The third address was up in the hills again, a commune.

The more cynical local citizens referred to these earnest young people as "Jesus freaks." They had left the urban squalor for cooperative community living. They grew organic vegetables that they sold at their store in town. Their hair was still long and they still wore the gaudy clothes of the sub-culture, but they had deserted all the evil opiates from nicotine to heroin and found new peace in the service of the Lord.

The young man we wanted was Peter Allis. We found him thinning out a patch of squash. He was wearing army fatigue trousers, thong sandals and a loose blouse of hopsacking.

His blond hair was down to his shoulders, his gray eyes had the luminous shine of the true believer. He was several inches over six feet tall, and muscular.

"I heard what happened," he told us. "If what I heard is true, she sinned. Suicide is a sin, in the eyes of God."

"We didn't ask for a judgment, Pete," Helms said gruffly. "If it hadn't been for Mrs. Marner, you wouldn't be here today."

"She didn't bring me here," the boy said quietly. "Our Savior brought me here."

"Did He come up with the seven hundred bucks to get you off the hard stuff? Mrs. Marner did."

"With the help of Jesus, she did." His chin lifted.

Helms shrugged, and looked at me. I asked, "When was the last time you saw her?"

"About a week ago. She thought I might know something about Jesus Gonzales."

"A week ago? He left town two weeks ago. Didn't Mrs. Marner know that?"

"She knew he had disappeared. She wasn't sure he had left town."

"And she came here to look for him? Are you a friend of his?"

"I was. Before I was cured, before I got the call. We went to high school together. We played football together." His face tightened. "Then he introduced me to drugs."

"To grass," Helms interrupted. "Only to grass, Pete."

The gray eyes glowed. "Marijuana, heroin, nicotine, alcohol, pills—they're all poison, aren't they? He introduced me to poison. Do friends do that to you?"

"Some friends might," Helms said. "Real friends, now, they hit their sons for seven hundred fish to put you into a clinic. When was the last time you saw Gonzales?"

"Almost two months ago. And he was still smoking—both cigarettes and marijuana. And he was still drinking beer."

"We'll have to start a file on him," Helms said dryly. "In five or six hundred years, it might be as thick as the file we have on you. Try not to get too holy, Pete. I have a weak stomach."

The boy's smile was beatific. "You can't make me angry, not anymore, Sergeant. I don't hate anymore."

"That's nice, real nice. What else did Mrs. Marner ask you about Gonzales?"

"Nothing. Did she really commit suicide, Sergeant?"

"We don't know. Back to the squash, Peter. Toil, son, for the night is coming."

We went past the community meeting hall and chapel toward the car. Helms said, "I liked him better when he was on horse. He was one tough kid."

"I take it you're not religious."

"I'm very religious. I worship in the temple of Mammon. How about you?"

"I was brought up as a Roman Catholic," I said. "I don't go to Mass anymore, but I guess I'm as much that as anything." I thought of the crucifix on Mrs. Gonzales's wall. "I got the impression from Mrs. Gonzales that she knew Jesus had left town. Do you know for sure?"

"I heard it. I didn't check it. If she reported him missing, the report is still down at the station. Should we head back?"

There were still some names on the list, but it had been a hot and tiring day. I nodded.

Mrs. Gonzales had reported her husband missing, but there were no additional details in the report. Nothing was reported about taking a bus out of town.

Helms asked, "Did you notice a phone when you were there?"

"I didn't. Let's look in the book."

There was no Vista Court Gonzales in the phone book. Helms asked, "Should we run over and talk with her?"

"Tomorrow. I've had enough for today."

He smiled. "That rich living has given you a sensitive stomach."

"I suppose. We're nowhere, aren't we? Maybe it *was* suicide."

He shrugged. "Maybe. But it's too early to tell the chief that. All of Maude's friends weren't poor, remember."

I took Main Street down to 101. We had the only traffic lights on this freeway between Los Angeles and San Francisco, which made it a way station for young wanderers.

They were lying on the grass between the sidewalk and the highway, with their packs and their signs. The signs read San Francisco and Monterey and San Jose. One comic gypsy was less specific. Anywhere but Here was chalked on his board.

They were mostly white and probably middle-class or higher. Old Karl Marx was wrong once again; the revolt had not come from the proletariat. It had come from the children of the merchant class he despised.

Nor had he foreseen labor unions riddled with hoodlums and supporting oppressive administrations. Nor the opiates for the masses that had supplanted the church: tv, the movies, dope. Karl would have made a lousy horseplayer.

The diesel trucks blatted along, fouling the air. The plastic punks in their overpriced sports cars darted in and out, changing lanes without clearance, pretentious innocents playing with bombs.

They peeled off at the Montevista ramp with the Cads and the Continentals. My old heap trailed behind, carrying a disgruntled and incompetent investigator home to his first booze of the day.

"I'll make them," Jan decided. "Then I'll know how much you're drinking."

I didn't argue.

"Nothing new," she guessed. "I can tell by your face."

"Nothing new that would make me happy," I said. "Make the drinks."

"In a minute. We're going over to Glenys's for dinner," she informed me. "Paul Pontius will be there."

I looked at her suspiciously. "You and Glenys haven't decided to play detective, have you?"

"Don't be silly. Paul has donated twenty thousand dollars to Glenys's pet charity. The least she can do is invite him to dinner. So don't you start on football with him, mister!"

"I promise you I will not start on *anything* with Paul Pontius. Get going on that drink—I want to take a shower."

"I'll make it. But before your shower, I want to hear about your day."

I started with Nowicki and worked my way through Vista Court and lunch with Juanita to Peter Allis. I mentioned the visit to Danning Villwock's mountain retreat, but eliminated the important thing he had told me.

"What does Juanita look like?" she asked me.

"She's a big woman, but I suppose some might find her attractive. She's about fifty years old. Her enchiladas are—well, almost up to yours."

"You meant better."

"Call it a draw."

She sat there on our twenty-seven-hundred-dollar sofa, and said, "Three babies and a mother in one room without a tub or shower?"

"In Los Angeles, I've seen eight in one room with a public toilet down the hall. I imagine we could see a lot worse in India."

"This isn't India."

"Not yet. Who else is going to be at the dinner?"

"Just Skip and June."

"Hasn't Glenys got a new man?"

"Not yet. But I'm helping her look."

I thought about Glenys while I took my shower.

A strange habit of mine, every time I take a shower my thoughts turn to women. It started in junior high school.

This Glenys was a tall, slim and elegant lady. The first and superficial impression one would get from her spinster attitudes on so many subjects was contradicted by her history.

She had been paired with some monumental studs when she lived in Beverly Hills, men who certainly weren't after her money. The only fortune hunter in the succession was the only man she had ever married. That marriage had lasted two days (and one night).

Her sister, June, was more standard, the sunny outdoor girl, the cheerleader type. Skip must have been the personification of all the college heroes she had rooted for. A dozen times since we had moved up here, she had told me how wonderful I had been to keep Skip out of jail—for her.

He, too, must have remembered the debt. He was standing in the entry hall when the butler opened the door. "I want to apologize, Brock," he said. "But jeepers, when I saw you standing there with Vogel—"

"I understood and so did Vogel. We were both wrong about him, Skip."

"One of us still is." He punched my arm. "Did you give up golf?"

"Temporarily. I decided I was too young to retire."

"Lay off, buddy. Each to his own. Anything new on Mrs. Marner?"

I shook my head.

"Why couldn't it be suicide? She had cancer, you know."

"According to the doctors. According to Maude

it was gas, from all that Mexican and kosher food she was always eating."

Then Glenys was coming to greet me. "My favorite vulgar person," she said, and kissed me. "Don't spill your cheap cigar ashes on my antique Kashan, shamus."

I would have topped her—if I could have thought of something. We went into the intimate little forty-foot living room. June Lund was in there, tanned and trim and smiling. And Mr. and Mrs. Paul Pontius.

I remembered him as gray haired and fat. He was about as fat as an N.F.L. center. On sober reappraisal he was gray haired and *big*.

He shook my hand and smiled. "Phyllis warned me not to mention football. But Skip told me you're the famous Brock the Rock. Even when I was a 49er fan, I admired you, sir."

"Thank you," I said. "Now that you've moved down here you might change your allegiance. This is going to be a Ram year."

"I'm afraid it is. You remember Phyllis, don't you, my wife?"

I remembered Phyllis. I hadn't been *that* drunk. She was red haired and statuesque, right out of the Folies Bergères, Las Vegas edition.

She gave me her glittering show-girl smile. "I remember you well, Brock," she said sweetly. "I hoped to see you sooner."

Two women in succession had left me without answers. "Thank you," I said humbly.

We sat and drank and talked about this and that, nothing worthy of recording. We ate fine food and drank fine wine (I guess) and went back to the living room for more talk.

Toward the end of the evening I was sitting next to Pontius, remote from the others, when he said quietly, "Would you drop in at my house tomorrow morning, Brock? Si told me you are working with the police on his mother's—on what happened."

"Glad to." I waited for more, for some clarifying statement.

None came. "Would nine o'clock be too early?" he asked.

"I'll be there."

9

IT HAPPENED around two o'clock in the morning. The first warning was the rattle of a glass on the tile of the bathroom-sink tile counter, about twelve feet from my unpillowed ear.

A prowler?

From the living room came the thump of a picture, bouncing against the wall.

Two prowlers?

No! The bed began to sway gently, back and forth. From the kitchen came the sound of rattling china. My heart pounded in my ears, as Jan crowded over, reaching for me blindly in the dark, whimpering words I can't remember now.

"Easy," I said quietly. "It will pass."

The bed stopped rocking and we untangled ourselves. I tried the bed-stand light. It worked. I snapped on the small radio to a flood of country music.

"No power lines down," I said. "At least not ours. It probably wasn't centered around here."

"It was close enough for me. The next one could be worse. Should we go outside?"

"Let's wait for the report."

The report interrupted the country music two aftershocks later. The quake had been centered off the coast of Oxnard, registering 4.7 on the Richter scale. No serious damage had been reported in the San Valdesto area; only scattered reports

of broken windows had been received from Oxnard so far. The possibility of a tidal wave was im-
minent along the Oxnard shore.

Nothing like an earthquake to remind a man of
his fragile mortality. We tried to get back to sleep,
but it was a nervous sleep, with only a few
snatches of oblivion.

We were up at six-thirty. "I'm not hungry," Jan
said. "How about you?"

"It's too early. I think I'll go over my notes. Why
don't you see if there's anything on the tube about
the quake?"

The local TV station was giving it the full treatment. They don't get too much earth-shaking
news in San Valdesto. Jan stayed with their repet-
itive coverage while I went over my Xerox copies,
trying to find a pattern or a clue. Nothing.

At eight o'clock, over our French toast, I said,
"Paul Pontius asked me to stop in and see him this
morning. I told him I'd be there at nine o'clock."

"Paul or Phyllis?"

I gave that the answer it deserved—silence.

"To put it in your vulgar terms, she's a lot of
mama, isn't she?"

"She has to be. He's a lot of man. Did you notice
how polite I was with him last night?"

"I did. Why does he want to see you?"

"He mentioned Maude, so maybe it's about that.
He might be the attorney for the estate."

"Joe Farini," she said, "is the Marners' attorney, and the Christophers'. Isn't he the attorney
who helped Skip that time?"

"He is. I thought he was strictly a criminal lawyer. He must have come up in the world."

The day was overcast and gloomy. The road that
led to the home of Paul and Phyllis Pontius wound
through an area of high stone fences and iron

gates, famous old estates now being unloaded on the new rich.

The Pontius place had been built years ago by a retired steel magnate. "Pittsburgh rococo" best described it. Every broken leaf, shell and scroll had been carefully restored.

I didn't see the inside. Paul Pontius was waiting for me outside, sitting on a wrought-iron bench in a small garden in the side yard.

"I'm still shaking," he said.

I sat on a wrought-iron chair near him. "I am, too. I got up at six-thirty."

"Phyllis is sleeping," he said. "She took some pills, but they're not for me." He paused. "Brock, in your line of work, I have to guess you know something about my background."

"I read the *Los Angeles Times*, if that's what you mean. A lot of people up here do. I didn't usually check people's backgrounds unless somebody paid me to do it."

"But if you read the piece in the *Times*, you'll remember that some of the men I defended had— doubtful connections."

"Two of them," I said, "were Mafia dons."

He smiled at me. "Are we going to fight again?"

"Not if you have friends in the Mafia, we're not."

"Brock, I'm an attorney, not a hoodlum. You've got to believe that: because what I'm going to tell you will look suspicious unless you do."

I returned his earlier smile. "Tell me and let me guess."

"Jesus!" he said. "You— All right! Those two men you mentioned, those alleged dons, now live in town here. They're old and they're retired and they certainly don't want any more trouble than they've already had with the law. But one of them told me something about a young friend who dropped in to see him when he was in town. The man was in town for a checkup at the Dolor Clinic here. He told my client about a prank he pulled for another friend in town, simply as a joke."

"Are you talking about a short, thin man who drives a yellow El Dorado?"

"I don't know what the man looks like or what he drives. He threatened some waitress downtown. Jan mentioned to Julie Marner that the police might have connected the incident to the death of Mrs. Marner."

"They're checking it. What was he, a hit man or just a muscle?"

"I have no idea."

The Dolor Clinic was popular with the Vegas boys. I asked, "Where was he from?"

"Nevada."

"Does the man have a name?"

"I don't know his name. And it's not a question I'm going to ask my client." He inhaled heavily. "Brock, believe me, there is only one reason I told you what I did. I want the police to find the murderer of Maude Marner as badly as you do. Si is probably my best friend. I told you this so the police won't waste their time on a blind alley."

"If they checked the Dolor Clinic, they could find out the man's name."

"Maybe. If he used his right name. We get a lot of Nevada patients at the Dolor Clinic, Brock."

"You're putting me in a bind," I said. "I'm supposed to be working with the police, but I can't reveal my source of this information. And you probably don't want me to tell them about the Dolor Clinic."

"I would appreciate that. I want to live here. I thought this was a favor I was doing you—and the police. I swear to you this man from Nevada had nothing to do with the death of Mrs. Marner. My client checked that out. The man was in Nevada the night Mrs. Marner was killed.''

"But what about his friend in town? Why did he want the waitress threatened? You called that a prank. It was no prank to the waitress. She was frightened enough to tell the police about it—and she's a part-time bookie.''

"Whoever the man in town was, he was a local. It's highly probable he has a record. Perhaps they had better question that bookie-waitress again and find out who she usually pays off to.''

"She doesn't pay. She's free-lance. That's why she was threatened.''

"Okay, there's your case. Find the payoff man. I can guarantee you he's local. My clients came here to die, not to operate.''

I sat there, thinking. "Okay, Paul," I said finally. "I'll take the police off that blind trail if I can. I won't mention your name or the clinic. If things get sticky and I have to, I'll come to you first and we'll figure out how to do it.''

"Fair enough," he said. "You have just made me a Ram fan.''

He might have honestly believed that hoodlum's threat against Mary Serano. It was also possible that, like Si, his relationship to the mob was peripheral. He had told me some dangerous information, information that could get him into trouble. Which meant he had trusted me—or he was working a ploy. He was a lawyer.

Then again, if he had really been involved with the mob except as an attorney, he would probably have been disbarred by now. No, that was a naive thought. When would I grow up?

I drove out his gate and past the other gates, be-

tween the pines and the live oaks and the eucalypti, past the Montevista Country Club, back to the
freeway and town.

Vogel was in Helms's office, using his type-
writer. Helms, he told me, would not be available
this morning. And then he asked, "What's this I
heard about Mary Serano? I can't find the report
here."

"Some creep threatened her." I paused, trying
to frame the right words. "He was from out of
town. I don't know his name. Don't ask for my
source."

His smile was thin. "Your old friend Juanita,
maybe?"

"Have you been checking my movements, Lieutenant?"

"Of course not. I didn't even know you'd seen
her. Did she tell you anything else?"

"She didn't even tell me that. But she promised
to keep an ear open. Though she is no Maude
Marner fan."

"I can guess. I've heard her on the subject of do-
gooders. She's a real free-enterprise woman, that
Juanita. Supported herself and most of her family
since she was twelve." He lighted a cigarette.
"And now for the question I'm not supposed to
ask—who told you about the out-of-town man?"

"No comment."

"A Vegas muscle, maybe?"

"Maybe worse. He wasn't very muscular, according to Mrs. Serano."

"He had a friend in town?"

I nodded.

"I can guess who the friend is, I'll bet."

"He had a couple of friends in town, but one
name my source didn't know and the other he
wouldn't give me. Let's just assume the local

friend could be the town payoff man. That's why Mary was threatened, because she doesn't pay off."

"Sure, sure. Great theory, no facts." He snuffed out his half-smoked cigarette in an ashtray. "You know where we are? We're nowhere!"

"So far. We're not quitting, are we?"

"Not according to Chief Harris. Back to the treadmill. Got any more names on the list of Marner's?"

"A few. But I think that first we should talk to Mrs. Gonzales again."

"Okay. That was some shake this morning, wasn't it?"

"It was. The next one could be worse. Is there such a thing as earthquake insurance?"

"If you're willing to accept a big deductible. I've got it. Let's go."

If we had been a few minutes later, we would have missed Mrs. Gonzales. There was an ancient stake truck parked in the alley in front of her second-floor apartment. Two wide-backed kinsmen were loading her furniture.

One of them grinned at Vogel. "Hi, Loot. I ain't seen you in the poker game at Manny's lately."

"I like to play for cash," Vogel said. "I can get paper at a stationery store. Is Mrs. Gonzales moving?"

"Home to mama," the man said. "She's upstairs. Still looking for Jesus, Loot?"

"My people," Vogel said, "gave up on Him two thousand years ago."

We climbed the outside steps to her apartment. The door was open. The children were not in sight; they probably had already been transported to grandma's place. I hoped it was bigger than this one.

Mrs. Gonzales was packing dishes. She looked up fearfully. "You have news about Jesus? Bad news?"

Vogel shook his head and glanced at me. I said, "We were wondering how you knew your husband had left town. The report at the station isn't complete."

"Lenny Tishkin told me. He went with Jesus to the bus station."

"Do you have Tishkin's address?" Vogel asked.

She shook her head.

"I have it," I said. "It's one of the names on Si's list."

We went down the steps and out to the department car. "Tishkin," Vogel said. "I should know that name. It rings a bell."

"Villwock," I said, "told me yesterday that Lenny Tishkin was the nastiest one of the kids on the list."

"Villwock? How would he know? He wasn't much more than a clerk, and not a very good one, at that."

"I thought he was a parole and probation officer."

"It's the same thing. Well, we can check Tishkin's record later. What's that address again?"

I gave it to him. We rode in silence for a few blocks before I said, "You're quite a shark at poker, I hear."

"Not good enough to keep me from day labor, or let my wife stay home. She isn't really crazy about that library work, now that kids no longer read."

"The way I heard it, you and Marner and Pontius are about the best in town."

"Huh! If they'd let me play with them more than once or twice a year, I could buy a house up in your neighborhood."

He stopped for a light at Main Street. "Marner tell you about my poker?"

"Nope. Helms."

He sat there, staring moodily ahead.

"The light has changed," I informed him. "Bad day, Bernie?"

"They're all bad," he said. "When do cops have good days? And every year it gets worse." He turned left on Main Street. "I remember that Tishkin now. Tough little bastard, a cinch for the gas chamber, eventually." He snorted. "Unless Nowicki and his knee-jerk liberal friends keep it from becoming law again."

If anybody, I thought, should be opposed to gas chambers, it should be you, Lieutenant Bernard Vogel. I said, "Nowicki and his friends will lose, Bernie. We live in a vindictive age."

The address I had for Leonard Tishkin was a few steps up from the Gonzales neighborhood, a cluster of cheap, fairly new stucco apartments between the freeway and the sea.

The manager repeated the familiar story. Lenny Tishkin had moved on. There was a slight variance this time; his rent had been fully paid.

"Did he leave a forwarding address?" Vogel asked.

The man shook his head. "Not with me. Maybe with the post office. Though he never got any mail that wasn't addressed to 'occupant.' "

"Occupant," Vogel muttered, as we walked back to the car. "That's what we all are, occupants. Faceless, nameless occupants."

I didn't argue with him. I had been carrying the same thought around with me all morning, ever since the earthquake.

10

I'VE FORGOTTEN the name of the last man we visited, but he checked out clean. He was working, his wife informed us. He would be home at four o'clock and would phone us then.

It was close to noon when we drove back to headquarters. Vogel went to another room to check the file, if any, on Tishkin; I sat in Helms's empty office reflecting on the morning's work. We knew little more now than we had when we started.

The file on Tishkin was slim: thirty days in a youth camp for marijuana possession, six months' probation for disturbing the peace. He had been acquitted of the most serious charge, robbing a liquor store. His alleged partner in the indictment had been Jesus Gonzales.

"Nowicki defended both of them," Vogel said. "Maybe we ought to talk with him."

"After the service," I suggested. "Are you going to Maude's memorial service?"

He nodded. "You going with your wife?"

"Nope. She's going with the Marners. Come on, I'll buy you your lunch."

"Today," he said, "I buy. I owe you."

I had expected something in the hamburger line, but he took me to the University Club. The way he explained it, he made enough, playing gin rummy with the members, to more than meet his monthly dues. It would have cost him money *not* to belong.

Over the martinis I said, "I was thinking of something a while ago. I was thinking that none of the other occupants of Kelly's Kourt would get this much attention if they had died under mysterious circumstances."

"You sound like Nowicki."

"Well, would they?"

"No unsolved murder case is ever considered closed."

"I'm talking about *active* investigation, Bernie. So what does a smart murderer do?"

"I don't know. I never met one."

I plowed on. "He figures that if he can make it look like suicide, however crudely, you boys will have an out."

"You boys? You mean the department?"

"I mean any understaffed and overworked police department headed by a politically minded chief."

"That would be almost all of them."

"Probably. Now, with the possibility of suicide still valid, the investigation comes to a dead end." I paused. "Where we are right now? We've had three and a half days of full department investigation and come up with zilch. When do you figure the chief will give his official pronouncement of suicide to the press?"

"Certainly not until Nowicki's friends get off his back."

"And then it will be called suicide and forgotten."

"It won't be forgotten."

"Come on!"

He said stiffly, "There have been murderers apprehended long after they thought they were in the clear."

"How many?"

"I don't know and neither do you. What's your point? Maude's dead. If she was murdered, and the murderer punished, she would be just as dead. Are you joining the vindictive age you were running down this morning?"

"I guess. It looks that way. But it really burns me to think that the son of a bitch who murdered Maude Marner is still breathing free air. I suppose that's adolescent emotionalism."

He nodded. "You must be a lousy poker player."

"The worst," I admitted. "I'll have another martini."

We left the car on the University Club parking lot and walked to the memorial service at the Unitarian church three blocks away. There was not a single empty parking space in the three blocks. Maude's friends had come early and come in force.

Si's and Julie's friends were there, about three dozen of them. Maude's friends filled the rest of the church and the foyer and the walled courtyard in front. The sweet odor of burning grass was strong in the courtyard; the lost children had come down from their mountain retreats and brought their own suckling children with them.

"The hope of tomorrow," Vogel muttered. "God help us!"

Chief Harris had saved us some seats in the last row. Helms was with him and two officers I hadn't met.

I told Helms, "That man who threatened Mary Serano was from out of town. I don't know his name."

"Where'd you learn that?"

"I can't tell you. And what I did tell you is all I know about him."

"Why muscle Mary? If the big boys are trying to

move in, they wouldn't start with her, would they? They'd start with the heavy money books."

"Maybe they already have those."

"No way. Remember, you're working with the department, Callahan. Your sources are our sources."

"Nope. The chief labeled me, Joe. I'm a citizen observer. My source told me the man had absolutely nothing to do with the death of Mrs. Marner."

"Maybe, maybe not. We'll talk about this later."

The crowd was quieting. The room was full. There was no altar in this church, the first I had visited in twenty years. There was no display of the body. Maude was now ashes, drifting through the rolling waters of the Pacific.

In one of the rows near the front, Jan was sitting with the Marners, Glenys and the Lunds. A few rows in front of us, the retired parole officer, Danning Villwock, sat with Nowicki.

The eulogy was fairly brief and quoted mostly from Emerson. Ralph Waldo Emerson, son of a Unitarian minister, had been a preacher too, in his earlier years.

Reason and the rational inquiry, that is the Unitarian bag. But the minister delivering the eulogy was young and he obviously had been a friend of Maude. There was no way he could keep the emotion from his voice.

He finished with four lines from "Good-bye":

> I laugh at the lore and the pride of man,
> At the sophist schools and the learned clan;
> For what are they all in their high conceit,
> When man in the bush with God may meet?

As we walked out, Vogel said in his cynical way,

"I wouldn't call Kelly's Kourt the bush, would you? I'm not even sure that Maude believed in God."

I had no learned answer, only a memorable line from Buddy Hackett I'd heard on TV. "It doesn't matter," I said. "I'm sure God believed in her."

The cars went away, carrying the mourners back to their labors or back to their hills, according to their life-styles. Chief Chandler Harris stood on the sidewalk, flanked by Nowicki and Helms, waiting for us.

"I think we should have a conference," he said, "in my office. I think we should coordinate what we have and determine where we are."

I nodded. Helms nodded. Nowicki said, "I'm free."

"So is your guilty client," Vogel said bitterly. "You are really a cute one, Stan."

Nowicki smiled. "I know. My mother has been telling me that for years."

Harris glared at both of them. "In my office. In twenty minutes."

They drove away. Vogel and I walked back to the University Club lot. "A conference," I said. "And then the official word—suicide."

"Don't bet on it."

"That old fox was counting the house," I said. "He saw how the unwashed outnumbered the washed."

"I know him better than you do," Vogel said, "and I'll tell you something. He may cut a corner here and there and he has to be a politician, but he's something better, too. He's all cop!"

"Seven bucks to a fin it's suicide."

"You've got a bet," he said.

Harris was in his chair behind his desk when we entered his office. Helms sat in a straight chair nearby. Nowicki was standing gazing out at the impressive view of bail bond offices across the street.

The chief held up a stack of papers about two inches thick. "Reports," he said. "All we know about the death of Mrs. Marner. Do you know what they add up to?"

All of us except Nowicki nodded.

"Do you now?" Harris grated. "All three of you agree on what they add up to? Would one of you Hawkshaws inform me?"

"They add up to nothing in the middle of nowhere," Vogel said.

Harris shook his head. "It's more serious than that. They add up to bad police work. It includes the most superficial coroner's report I have ever seen, and I've seen some beauts from that office. All he tells us is that the lady died from carbon monoxide poisoning. If one of our meter maids had found Mrs. Marner's body, she could have guessed that."

He stopped to get his breath, his face glowing.

"Was there any indication that the lady had been bound or gagged? Any rope marks on her body, any lint on her teeth or in her mouth, any evidence of a fight for life? No mention of it here." He slapped the papers on his desk. "And no mention of the lack of it here!"

Vogel said, "He was questioned about it. He said he hadn't noticed any."

"After the body was gone, after it was cremated, he was questioned about it. He hadn't noticed any? Had he *looked* for any? Was he asked that question?"

Vogel nodded. "I asked him. He only repeated that he hadn't noticed any. He's not a detective, Chief."

"On this kind of case he is supposed to be. And now Gonzales. Mrs. Marner was asking around about him, the reports show. What did we originally have on him? An incomplete missing persons report. Here's a kid who finally straightened out. Got himself a fair job, a better than fair future, *finally*. Is that the kind of man who suddenly takes a bus out of town? Was there any checking of the original report? Hell, no!"

He was breathing heavily now, and his red face was glowing like a neon sign. "Why not?"

Nobody answered.

"Maybe," the chief went on in a softer but even meaner voice, "we *knew* Gonzales had left town because Lenny Tishkin told us so. Is that the place to get the official word, from a vicious punk who started to lie when he started to talk?"

"He was Gonzales's best friend," Helms said.

"Was he?" The chief looked at Nowicki.

"At one time," Nowicki said. "Not in the last year. Tishkin went one way and Jesus another. And Lenny resented it. You can be sure of one thing—Lenny Tishkin didn't go to the bus station with Gonzales unless he had a massive change of heart in the past month."

"But if Lenny killed Jesus," Harris said, "and Maude Marner suspected it—"

"That's a real wild guess, Chief," Vogel interrupted quietly. "That's completely unsubstantiated speculation."

"Hell, yes," Harris admitted. "But it's a line of inquiry, isn't it? Do we have a bulletin out for Tishkin?"

Vogel shook his head. "There was no basis for it."

"There is now. Get it out." He looked at each of us in turn. "Do any of you really think a woman attempting suicide would take the trouble to fasten a seat belt?''

Nobody answered. Nobody knew, including the man who had asked the question.

"But one way to keep a dead body upright in a car seat is to strap her in, isn't it? If a man's in a hurry to leave, that's a quicker way to take her home and leave in a hurry, isn't it?''

Again, nobody answered.

He stood up and pushed back his chair. "The rest of you can leave now. I want to talk with Mr. Callahan for a few minutes.''

They went out and closed the door. He stood there for a few seconds, arching his back and rubbing his neck. "I'm getting old,'' he said, "old and achey and impatient.''

"You don't have an easy job,'' I said. "Not these days.''

He nodded. "But I didn't keep you behind to talk about my health. What you are doing, working with us, is very unusual police practice, I'm sure you know.''

"It's rare,'' I agreed. "Though I've done it in Los Angeles, when I was active.''

"And when you worked with them down there, the cooperation was complete, wasn't it?''

"On my side,'' I said. "There was, of course, information that they didn't share with me.''

"Have we kept any information from you?''

I smiled at him. "Chief, we're working our way east too slowly. Let's go all the way to Vegas. I don't know the man's name. I only got that probably meaningless piece of information because I promised the source complete secrecy.''

"One question. Was it Silas Marner?''

I shook my head. "I swear to you it wasn't. And I can't see any Vegas angle here. They're not that tricky, that complicated. They're quick and dirty."

"And all over the country," he added.

I thought a moment, and said, "Right. Including here, a couple of them pretty big wheels in the mob."

He stared at me. "Who told you that?"

"Nobody," I lied. "It's kind of complicated, the way I found out."

"I have the time."

"Well, a classmate of mine at Stanford lives down in Los Angeles. But at one time his family owned a lot of property in this town, going way back. He had the mistaken idea that they still had claims to some of that property where the condominiums were built out there near the university. Even if he didn't have a legitimate claim, he thought he might pick up a few dollars by threatening them with a flawed title. He hired me to make a title search, which I did. Right up to the present buyers. And that's where I saw the names."

He nodded wearily. "They're here. Before they moved here to retire, their attorney came in and promised me there would be no mob action in this town."

"He probably told the truth," I said. "You can't stop a man from retiring here."

"And it's hard to stop a working man from working, not when there's money in it. I'm older than you are, so you probably don't know the days when all those retired clothing manufacturers retired in Los Angeles, most of them New Yorkers."

"That was before my time," I said.

"They couldn't stand loafing," he said. "They didn't know how. So they started up with some small factories. And now Southern California is the leading area for women's sports clothes in America."

"They did it for the money," I said. "In San Valdesto there's probably a lot more money in real estate than in drugs or gambling."

"Those clothing men didn't need the money. They needed action. What if these boys get the itch to be active again? If they decide to move in, we're not big enough or smart enough to stop them."

"No town is today, Chief. Because the citizens don't give a damn. There aren't enough Maude Marners left."

"Amen," he said.

11

Vogel was waiting for me in the hall. "Seven dollars please?"

I handed him a five and two ones.

"What did he want with you? You were in there long enough."

"Oh, we discussed strategy and sophisticated detection techniques."

"I'll bet. Did you tell him the name of your source?"

"No. You were right about him. He's all cop."

"A little on the imaginative side at times. That Tishkin-Gonzales script might sell in Hollywood."

"But you didn't buy it?"

"I don't usually assume murder until I find a dead body. Maybe I've been in this business too long and learned to rely on routine. And I don't enjoy getting dressed down."

"He's getting old, Bernie. And achey and impatient."

"Who isn't? Helms has gone over to have another talk with Mrs. Gonzales. Have you got any bright ideas, or should we sit and play gin rummy for three months while we wait for a response to that bulletin?"

"Gonzales must have had some friends worth questioning besides Peter Allis and Tishkin. Do you know of any?"

He shook his head. "Nowicki might. But he's left. Should I call his office?"

"Why don't I stop in there on the way home? You can check out what you might have here. Those martinis you bought me have dulled my brain."

"Okay," he said wearily. "See you tomorrow."

Nowicki's office was closed. He was probably in court. Working men were still working. I wasn't a working man. I was a wealthy amateur, an outsized Lord Peter Wimsey, a brainless Peter Wimsey. But it was too early to go home. The going-home traffic was too light to let me impersonate a working man.

I went to the club and put on my spikes and took a big bucket of balls over the practice range. Plunk, plunk, plunk, smothered hooks and wild slices, tops, shanks and dribblers.

And then I smashed one, a two-iron that soared into orbit, straight and clean as the search for truth. It takes time and work and attention to detail to hit one that clean.

Time and work and attention to detail had made Jack Nicklaus rich and Bernie Vogel cynical. How else can a cop work? His instincts, or even a confession, can assure him a man is guilty, but a court will make the decision, not the cop.

In court Perry Mason can put all the intricate pieces together and confront the guilty man with a faultless mosaic—and the criminal will break down and slobber his confession. But if you think suspects break down and confess, you haven't spent much time around criminal courts. Suspects break down and confess about as often as there are heat waves in Antarctica.

Maybe I've been in this business too long and learned to rely on routine.

How else, Bernie? How else can you keep the tigers out of our patios? Time and work and attention to detail.... The daily grind, the daily round-up, the records, the dossiers, the bulletins, the interrogations and snitches and deals and compromise settlements. How else? You're a working man, Bernie. Your nose is too big for TV and you lack the gift for persuasive fraudulence.

Skip Lund came over from the pro shop with a bag of balls. "Well, well, look who's here! The working man in his moment of leisure."

"Go clip another coupon," I said.

He smiled at me doubtfully. "You still hot about that Vogel business?"

"No. I'm sorry. How's everything with you?"

"Dull. June and I are going over to Hawaii for a week to get away from those Fiesta tourists headed for town." He spilled out his bag of balls. "You're sure getting grouchy lately, old buddy."

"It will pass. So will we. Keep your head down and follow through, golden boy."

I could feel his eyes on me as I carried my clubs back to the pro shop. I was embarrassed. Probably, if I had been born with his throwing arm, with his disarming smile and agile body and handsome face, I would not have earned the pedestrian nickname of the Rock. There was no reason to resent him; I had some playboy tendencies myself. I simply lacked his equipment.

Jan wasn't home. The liquor cabinet beckoned, but I headed for the refrigerator and a bottle of Einlicher.

Despite Vogel's scorn for it, the chief had given us a line of inquiry. Murder has too many motives. With larceny it's money, with rape it's lust and violence. Those are clear trails. The motives for murder are less obvious. The chief had waded through all that paper and come up with a purely speculative pattern. What else did we have?

I was dozing when Jan came home. I half heard her making noises in the kitchen and clinking bottles in the den. She came into my line of vision in the living room. She had a martini in her hand.

"I won't ask," she said, "because the answer is either 'nothing' or 'nowhere.' "

"You are very perceptive for a retired interior decorator. How was your day?"

"The memorial service was probably the high point. You looked gloomy, sitting there with all those policemen."

"It has been a gloomy day. What's for dinner?"

"Nothing of interest. I suppose I could warm up some leftovers. Let's eat out."

"All right. Is it too soon for Mexican food again?"

"Not for me. Did you plan to introduce me to your Juanita?"

"I'll say it again—you're very perceptive."

We took my car. Jan's Mercedes, I figured, would stay in one piece for about twelve minutes on Rivera Street. We took the freeway to Padilla turnoff, and Padilla Street to Rivera.

A gray Maserati had pulled in behind us on Padilla, and turned left when we did on Rivera. There was a parking space in front of Juanita's place, which I took.

We were getting out of the car when I saw the Maserati make a U-turn at the next corner. We were going up the steps to the restaurant when I saw it pull into a parking space across the street.

"And you worried about my little Mercedes," Jan said. "That thing cost twice as much."

"Maybe the driver lives down here."

"With a car like that? Why would he live here?"

"Because," I told her, "this is where the action is."

There were three men at the bar, one of them an Anglo. There were about a dozen people in the dining room, more than half of them Anglo. Juanita would have an "in" place yet, if she didn't get tired of cooking. A tall, thin black man was behind the bar; she was probably in the kitchen.

I told the waitress, "If Mrs. Rico is in the kitchen, will you tell her Callahan has brought his bride in, as he promised he would?"

She nodded. "Would you like a drink?"

Jan shook her head. I said, "A stein of Einlicher."

Juanita arrived about a minute after the beer, smiling, wiping her hands on her apron, appraising Jan.

"No wonder I lost out," she said. "You are a very attractive woman, Mrs. Callahan."

"Thank you. I hope you'll have time to eat with us, so my husband doesn't sulk."

Juanita nodded. "In a few minutes. Enchiladas, Pancho?"

I shook my head. "I can get enchiladas as good as yours at home. You decide what we should eat."

"I'll be back as soon as I make myself presentable." She went to the kitchen.

We had chicken chalupas and chili rellenos and refried beans. We had some laughs and a three-person rapport. It was close to eight o'clock when Juanita glanced around her almost full room and said, "Look at all the gringos here. I'll have to raise my prices."

I asked, "Have you been keeping your ears open?"

She stiffened. "Is this the time to talk about that?"

I nodded.

She looked at Jan. "What a thing you married, snoop, snoop, night and day. Is business all he ever thinks of?"

"I'm not raising *my* prices," I told her. "What happened, Juanita?"

"You are working with the police," she said quietly. "I had this list made out before I learned that. Some of the people on the list are friends of mine but not friends of the police."

"So you tore up the list?"

She shook her head. She glanced toward the bar. I followed her gaze to see an enormous black man in a white linen suit staring at her. She looked back at me.

"Is he on your list?" I asked.

She looked at me, at Jan, and past us both. "The man at the bar is no friend of mine. He is on the list. His name is Otis Locum. He is not a man you should trifle with."

"What's his business?"

"Girls. All colors, all ages, mostly kids. He is a very dangerous man, Pancho."

Jan said, "Let's go, Brock. I'm frightened, I don't like this."

"No need to go because of him," Juanita said quietly. "Nothing will happen in here. Mr. Locum knows I, too, have friends. But I want to take some of their names off the list. I thought you were private."

"I might have to be, if the police give up on this. Could you phone me, later? I'll be up."

She nodded. "And now let us pretend to be enjoying ourselves. Couldn't we laugh a little?"

"We don't have to," I said. "Mr. Locum has left."

"No, he hasn't," Jan said. "He's talking on the wall phone at the end of the bar."

"To hell with him," Juanita said. "Another Einlicher, Brock? And maybe a liqueur, Mrs. Callahan?''

"Fine," I said.

"Call me Jan," my bride said.

It had been an overcast day. When we left half an hour later it was an overcast night, not a star in sight. On the side of the street, about half a block away, a big blob of white was standing next to what looked like a camper, one of the kind that is slid over the box of a pickup truck.

A car came along the street toward us. Its headlights illuminated the bulk of Otis Locum, leaning in, apparently talking to the driver of the camper. I couldn't see the license plate.

I told Jan, "I'm going to make a U-turn. When we drive past that camper down there, I want you to get the license number. Your eyes are better than mine."

"All right," she said. "But let's get out of here. I'm frightened, Brock!"

I was halfway through the U-turn when the camper pulled away. I goosed the rear end around, the tires squealing, as Jan gasped. I must have been up to thirty—before I had to jam the brakes.

Otis Locum stood in the middle of the street, smiling into our headlights, the front bumper about twelve feet from where he stood.

He came around to my side of the car, still smiling. My window was half-open; he put one big hand on the top edge of the glass. "What's your hurry, whitey?"

"I wanted to check out your friend," I told him. "Take your hand off the glass before you lose it."

"You a cop or something? I don't see no red light."

"I'm not in the red-light business. You've got exactly three seconds to save your hand."

"Brock," Jan whispered. "Please, Brock, let's go."

Locum grinned—and took his hand off the glass. "The little lady is right. Just go, whitey. This is a *mean* neighborhood." He waved, and walked over to a gray Maserati parked at the curb.

The Mustang moved on. "You're absolutely crazy!" Jan said. "He must weigh three hundred pounds!"

"Josh Leddy of the Green Bay Packers weighed three hundred and seven pounds. I put him out for the season with a broken leg."

"Two hundred years ago. You're crazy, completely crazy."

I put a hand on her knee. "I know. It was crazy. But I hate men who deal in girls. Because I love girls. Maybe we could find that camper if we scouted around."

"Take me home first and then do your damned scouting!"

Back to the freeway, back to Montevista, back to the fringe cottage with no further dialogue.

There, Jan said, "I'm going to bed. I've got a headache."

"I'm sorry I acted so crazy."

"It's not that. I really do have a headache. I know it's Saturday night and all, but—"

I kissed her forehead. "I believe you. Take some aspirin. I'm going to sit up and wait for Juanita's phone call."

I was sorry to see her go to bed without me. Up until the Locum confrontation, it had been an increasingly romantic evening. There was no way I would be able to get to sleep for a while, not with the anticipation I had been nursing through the last hour.

I turned on the tube, but it was all garbage. I

phoned Juanita's place to tell her about what had happened in the street half a block from the restaurant, wanting to ask her if she knew who the man in the camper could have been.

But she had left for the night. Perhaps she would phone me from home.

I sat for an hour, sulking, before going to bed. I didn't visit our connubial bed. I took a blanket out of the linen closet and slept on the couch in the den.

I could have headaches, too.

12

THE FAT SUNDAY *Los Angeles Times* was on the lawn, chewed by a neighbor's dog. The local paper was unspoiled; this particular dog had a provincial hatred for the *Times*.

I had thawed out some of the Danish pastry we had bought in Solvang and started the percolator before Jan came into the breakfast room.

She asked, "What time did Juanita call?"

"She didn't."

She stared at me doubtfully. "Do you think—" She didn't finish.

"It's possible she's scared or she could have been busy. I'm sure nothing has happened to her. I'll find out tomorrow. How's your headache?"

"Gone. But I'm tense. I had some of the damnedest nightmares. I thought, when we moved up here, all those crazy things you got involved in down in Los Angeles would be behind us."

"They are. Do you want me to quit?"

"I wouldn't think of telling you what to do. Did you take the sweet rolls out of the freezer?"

"They're on the kitchen counter. I warmed the oven. Jan, if it had been anybody but Maude—"

"All right, all right," she said. "I'm too weary to argue. Did you get both papers?"

"Yes, ma'am. Go on with your household duties. I'm reading about my Rams."

"Rah, rah, rah," she said. "Sis, boom, bah!"

I read on, against the background noises of clink, clank, splash and gurgle. And then a silence. And then she was back in the breakfast room, glaring at me.

"How can you sit there and read about those dumb Rams when you haven't the faintest idea of what happened to Juanita?"

"Sit down, emotional child," I said, "and I will tell you about Juanita."

She went to the kitchen to pour herself a cup of coffee and came back to sit down across from me.

"Do you remember," I asked her, "when I had my only case in this town? Do you remember the trouble Skip was in, and how he went into hiding, and I had to come up here and talk some sense into him?"

She nodded.

"After I got Skip to come out of hiding, the local police tried to implicate him in a murder. That's when I met Vogel. They almost did it, too. But I found the real murderer for them."

"What does all this have to do with Juanita?"

"The real murderer was Juanita's husband. And right in that bar where Locum stood last night, her husband tried to shoot me with a great big .45-caliber Colt. He would have, too."

I took a deep breath, remembering.

"Go on!"

"Juanita saved my life. She emptied both barrels of a twelve-gauge shotgun into her hubby's stomach. He was never reassembled for the funeral. He had to be mopped up."

She was staring at me now, glassy eyed.

"So you see," I went on patiently, "it's not the Juanitas of this world I worry about. It is all those fifteen- and sixteen-year-old runaways—girls that Locum and his friends are probably converting into prostitutes. This is a tourist town, a convention town, and what is a convention without call girls?''

"I don't want to hear any more.''

"Then I'll shut up. But next time don't ask me why I wanted to take my chances with a man as big as Otis Locum. I was *aching* to take my chances with that puke.''

"All right, all right.'' She stood up. "I'll get breakfast. The pastry should be warm enough by now.''

Over the pastry and scrambled eggs and coffee, she asked, "Did you plan to go to the match with me this afternoon?''

"What match?''

"At the tennis club. June's in the county finals.''

"Honey! The Rams are playing an exhibition game with the 49ers, and it's on the tube.''

"Okay. Skip will pick me up, then. I'll go with him and June.''

Skip came to pick her up around noon. He was driving a brand-new camper, only a week old. He insisted I go out to admire it. He pointed out all the features that fascinated him and bored me, the ample propane stove and oven, the comfortable beds, the fiberglass shower.

"It's very nice,'' I said. "I had dinner with one of your old friends last night.''

"Which one?''

"Juanita Rico. Seen her lately?''

He shook his head. "I don't hang around that neck of the woods anymore. How is she doing?''

"Very well. She's starting to get the carriage trade. You shouldn't forget your old friends.''

"She was never that close a friend.''

"She saved my life,'' I explained, "so I have a different relationship with her.''

He smiled. "Yes, Father Callahan. Do you know what you are? You're an anachronism. You're right out of one of those old Humphrey Bogart movies."

"Probably. And you've become the playboy of the western world. At least I'm consistent."

"A foolish consistency," he said, "is the hobgoblin of little minds. Emerson, Ralph Waldo."

Nothing from me.

"I grew up and faced reality," he said.

"You certainly did. And it's done wonders for your backswing."

He laughed. "Brock, you're crazy. I love you, but you're crazy."

He was probably right. How could I be so out of tune with so many people and still be sane. . . .

The camper went away, carrying my love, and I went back into the house. The Einlicher smiled at me, but I made myself a double martini and settled in front of the tube.

I watched the last quarter of the Jets-Patriots game from New York, and then went to the kitchen to fry some kosher weiners and get some olives. I consumed them with four slices of sourdough toast and three glasses of milk. I brought another martini back to the tube with me in time for the kickoff.

Every season, the Rams would play the 49ers three times, two official games, one exhibition. Almost every year, the Rams would win all three games. But the 49ers had taken two of the three last year, and were supposed to be even better this season.

This game reasserted the Rams' dominance. This was a solid club. We now had a quarterback more concerned with moving the team than with getting quotes into the press.

We had a new owner and a new coach who knew football was played on the field, not in the news media. They had traded for some hard-nosed boys who had grown up to know that they weren't getting their kind of pay to impress reporters.

It was still the third quarter, but the game was in the bag, when the phone rang.

It was Juanita. "I had nothing to tell you last night, so I didn't call. And I have nothing now. My friends are also my customers. I want to talk with them first."

"Okay. When I went out last night, Locum was up the block a ways, talking with somebody in a camper. Do you know who it could have been?"

"No."

"Does Locum come into your place often?"

"Not often. He knows I don't like him. Why do you ask?"

"Because I have a feeling he was only there because I was. It's possible he went out to report my presence to the man in the camper. He used your phone a few minutes before he left."

"It could be. Pancho, are you angry with me?"

"We all have to make a living. I am a little disappointed. I'll keep in touch."

She had a business now and was getting the gringo trade. She would be joining the Better Business Bureau one of these days. These were the sour thoughts I had, poisoned by the martinis. They always affected my chemistry. One I could handle. More than one turned me paranoiac.

I turned off the game and went to the bathroom to take a shower. Hot, hot and hotter, numbing the frayed nerve ends. No feminine fantasies today; I saw the smiling face of Otis Locum.

June Lund had won her match. She was now the champion female player of San Valdesto County.

That might not seem monumental to a citizen of Peru, but she was the only person in the world who could officially make that statement.

She and Skip, Glenys and some man whose name I have forgotten, came home with Jan to celebrate the victory. The martinis had already poisoned me; I nursed an Einlicher through the bedlam.

Chitchat, persiflage, gossip and merriment, filling the void of the days before the big sleep.

They left around nine o'clock, and Jan asked, "Well, hermit, what did your Rams do?"

"I'm sure they won. I didn't see the finish. Juanita phoned. She wants more time with her list."

"Do you think that man, that Locum, frightened her?"

"I don't know. She told me her friends are her customers. It could be a purely business decision."

Jan nodded without interest and began picking up ashtrays and glasses carrying them back to the kitchen. When she returned to the living room she seemed dispirited.

"What's wrong?"

"I feel so—so useless. Everybody here can play tennis or golf or sail boats or ride horses. I feel so useless—physically."

"I could teach you to wrestle," I offered. "Why don't we go into the bedroom and I'll teach you how to wrestle?"

"Let's go," she said.

13

THE WIND HAD SHIFTED. The sun came up glaring on Monday morning. Sergeant Helms was in his office, staring out the window.

"Do you know a man named Otis Locum?" I asked him.

"I do. He's been picked up more times than a girl hitchhiker. But we could never make anything stick. Where did you hear about him?"

I related my Saturday-night adventure.

"Get the license number of the camper?"

I shook my head.

"What color was it?"

"I couldn't tell for sure. It was light colored. I'm a little color blind between blue and green. It might have been either. From a distance it looked like one of those conversions on a pickup truck."

He studied me sourly. "You weren't going to tangle with Locum unarmed, were you?"

"You're making noises like my wife. I've crippled bigger men and they were wearing pads. If you remember Josh Leddy of the Packers—"

"Never heard of him, footballer. And there's no referee on the field where Locum plays." He turned back to the window and stared out again.

"You look unhappy, Sergeant."

"I didn't enjoy the chief's lecture. I've been wondering if there isn't an easier way to earn fifteen hundred and twelve dollars a month."

"Take-home pay?"

"Huh! I take home enough for a pound of ground meat. What were you doing down at Chickie's?"

"Eating Mexican food and introducing Juanita to my wife. Locum's a pimp, the way I heard it."

"Locum's anything that will turn a dirty buck. But try to prove it. You know what one of those Maseratis costs?"

"More than fifteen hundred and twelve dollars, I'm sure. Is he the big man in town?"

"This town is full of big men. I guess he's about the biggest crooked man in town, at least down there." He went to his desk, opened a drawer and took out a package of cigarettes. "I've got to give a talk at Marquez High summer school this morning. You'll probably work with Vogel. He's in with the chief now."

"You should get a bonus," I told him, "for all the public-relations work you do."

"Start a petition," he said. "See you later."

Saturday's *Times* was still on his desk. I had read today's sports pages at breakfast. I turned to the financial pages to see what those sharpies on Wall Street had done to my money. They had kept me even for Friday, a new record. The D.J.I. had gone up almost eight points; I had only broken even.

I was still doodling on a scratch pad when Vogel came in. He looked at the doodles, at the financial page, and said, "Put your money into the Savings and Loan. Those New York bastards will destroy you."

"You've been burned," I guessed.

"All the ways there are. Helms gone?"

"He had a lecture date. Where do we go today?"

"We'll follow the chief's script until we get a better one. We could start with Nowicki. Did you talk with him Saturday?"

"No. He wasn't there."

"Maybe," Vogel suggested, "you could go in alone. Nowicki and I have this mutual animosity pact. I don't think he'd tell me which side he dresses on."

"With his politics? He'd have to dress on the left."

"Clever! Let's go."

I told him about Locum as we rode down Main Street and he said, "That could be an angle. Maude worried about her girls more than she did about boys. And girls are Locum's big business."

"Is that business big enough in this town to make him rich?"

"He can convert them here and ship them anywhere. The runaway kids are here. He came up from Los Angeles about nine years ago. We could never get a line on his connections, but he must have some big ones. He lives real high and he doesn't call Nowicki when we pick him up."

"Who does he call? Paul Pontius?"

"Pontius is retired. He doesn't mess around with this local trash. Locum calls Joe Farini. You got a thing about Pontius?"

"I remember all those hoods he got off in Miami."

"He's a lawyer. If they could afford him, they hire him. But that was before he retired."

Joe Farini had been Lund's lawyer. Vogel might have remembered that, or he might not have. In the interests of our new relationship, I decided not to remind him.

He stopped the car in front of Nowicki's office. "I'll wait here," he said.

Nowicki was speaking Spanish with a stout Mexican woman when I entered. A few English words broke through; she was evidently complaining about a local time-installment furniture store. "Cheaters" was the English word she used the most.

He walked to the door with her when they'd finished. When he came back to his desk, he was smiling. "Vogel your chauffeur?"

"He thought he might not be welcome."

"He's wrong. With Bernie, if you don't agree with him one hundred percent, you're his enemy. But I wish all cops were as straight as he is."

He shuffled through some papers and handed me a note-sized sheet. "These are the only names I could come up with that fit the chief's scenario. I don't think I'm breaking any attorney-client relationship." He smiled. "And a thousand-dollar donation should earn you a few extra privileges."

There were three names on the list, complete with address. "Thanks. Any ideas of your own, barrister? Any theories?"

He shook his head. "Only a dim hunch that Tishkin might be a key. But he's not the kind you can break down, if you find him. He's smart and he's tough. Villwock told me something at the service Saturday that might help. That second name on the list, Patty Serano, lived with Tishkin for almost three years."

"Any relation to the waitress, Mary Serano?"

"She's Mary's daughter. But she doesn't live at home. She's been on her own since she was fifteen."

The whole trip was a waste of taxpayers' gasoline. The two males were at work. It took us half the morning to learn where they worked, and they had nothing important to tell us about Lenny Tishkin when we finally tracked them down. The address for Patty Serano was the same address we had checked for Lenny, but we checked it again.

She, too, had moved on.

Vogel asked the manager, "How come you didn't mention her when we were here Saturday?"

"You didn't ask," the man said.

Vogel studied him coldly. "You know they weren't married, didn't you?"

"Are you for real? Half the kids living together today aren't married. A cop should know that. They paid their rent on time and they didn't throw loud parties. You get tenants like that, you don't bug 'em with dumb questions."

It had been a frustrating morning. Vogel continued to stare at the man.

"Let's go, Bernie," I said quietly. "Faceless, nameless occupants, that's all. Remember?"

Back in the car, he said, "So much for Nowicki's help." He sat behind the wheel, staring out at the street ahead.

"We could check Lund," I kidded him. "He was over to my house yesterday with his new camper. Maybe you could nail him this time."

He said harshly, "You overlook a lot of opportunities to keep your mouth shut, Callahan. Put your brain to work for a change and think of a place to go next."

"That liquor store," I suggested, "the one Gonzales and Tishkin were indicted for robbing. The way I read it in the file, the owner gave positive identification to the investigating officer, and then changed his story in court. Maybe by now he has his guts back."

"Maybe Nowicki bought him off. Maybe we ought to investigate Nowicki."

I kept my mouth shut.

"All right," he said, after a few seconds. "Do you remember the address?"

"I remember the name. Trinity Liquors. It's on Padilla Street."

We were halfway there when Vogel said, "What difference would it make if the man changed his mind? It wouldn't have anything to do with Maude, would it?"

"It could give us some leverage on Tishkin—if we ever find him."

"You're not making sense. Tishkin's already acquitted. What kind of leverage is that on a man we suspect of murder? Or the chief does."

"You suggested we follow the chief's script. Let's stick with it."

"You and the chief," he said, "should move to Hollywood."

The liquor-store owner hadn't changed his story; I had misread the file. His name was Moses Jones. He was black and short and thin and feisty.

"It was Gonzales and it was Tishkin," he told us. "You think those silly stockings over their heads fooled me? I know their builds, I know their voices. But that smart-ass lawyer of theirs made a monkey out of me in court. I'll tell you something else, officer, I'm not the only one those punks robbed."

"I'm sure you're not," Vogel agreed wearily. "But you don't have any evidence solid enough to stand up in court, do you?"

"That's for sure. What I got is two gutless competitors that know what I know. Manny Adler, over at A-1 Beverages, and Barney Leeds at Padilla Grog Shop. They told me, *privately*, what I'm telling you about Tishkin and Gonzales. You talk to them and they'll tell you I'm a liar."

Manny Adler, A-1 Beverages: "The man's crazy! I never told him anything."

Barney Leeds, Padilla Grog Shop: "Moses who? Don't know the man."

"Did you know Gonzales?"

"Half of my customers are named Gonzales. I don't remember that one."

Back on the sidewalk, I said, "Liars, both of them. Moses' place is only a block from here. And why would Moses lie about Adler?"

Vogel shrugged. "Who knows? Hungry?"

"I could eat. How about Chickie's?"

"Too hot for my ulcer. We'll go kosher today. You buy. It's your turn."

At Plotkin's Pantry, Vogel had borscht, gefilte fish and herring in sour cream, guaranteed to assuage his ulcer. I stayed on the safe side with two corned beef sandwiches and a gargantuan kosher pickle.

Over the best coffee I'd had in this town, Vogel lighted his ten-thousandth cigarette of the day and said, "You must be mental."

"Why?"

"Riding around like this, getting nowhere, when you could be living the good life. At least, win or lose, I get paid for it."

"There are other jobs that pay more with less work and less danger. How come you didn't choose one of those?"

"I don't know. But I guarantee you I wouldn't have gone to work for the department if they didn't pay."

"Your pa's delicatessen would have paid more. Your friend Plotkin, who runs this place, just bought the city a park."

"So we're both fools."

I finished my coffee. "Was Maude, too? She could have moved in with Si and lived like a queen."

"That's different," he said. "She helped people. I put them in the can. I think maybe I'm a vindictive type."

"Me, too," I said. "Let's look up Locum. Do you know where he hangs out?"

"I know a few of the places. And I know where he lives. We'll try his house first."

He lived high on a bluff above the sea, at the northern edge of town, as close to the exclusive Slope Ranch section as a black man was likely to get. The house was low and large, mostly antiqued redwood, with a fieldstone facing. The Maserati was parked in the concrete driveway.

Vogel parked behind it. "This could constitute harassment, I guess you know. And he's got an expensive lawyer."

"I know. I could ask the questions. The chief can't demote me."

"That's the way we'll play it. You're the concerned citizen. I'm only here because you insisted on it."

The door chimes went through their sequence twice, some tune I'd never heard before. Then the big man stood there, filling the doorway. He was arrayed in yellow flared slacks and a black and yellow striped tennis shirt.

His smile was broad and patronizing. "Well, Lieutenant Vogel! What have I done wrong now?"

"Nothing I know of," Vogel said. "This is Mr. Callahan, one of our local citizens. He has a complaint."

"We've met," Locum said curtly.

"Saturday night," I agreed. "You stood in the middle of Rivera Street and blocked my passage."

He frowned. "You must have been drunk, Mr. Callahan. I didn't block no passage. You almost ran me down, man!"

He looked at Vogel. "I stopped in at Chickie's for a drink. *One* drink, that's all, Lieutenant. When I went back to my car, this tourist, some cat in a camper, asked me how to get to Mission Drive. I told him, and started to walk back to my car—and whammo, this car of Mr. Callahan's is burning rubber and aiming right at me! Shakes a man up, thing like that, and maybe I got a little lippy. But hell, if anybody's got a beef, it's me, not him."

"I see. Could you describe the man in the camper?"

Locum scowled and shook his big head slowly. "It was dark, Lieutenant. He was white, I can tell you that much. Weighed maybe a hundred and forty, hundred and fifty. Is he important or something?"

"He could be involved in prostitution," Vogel said blandly. "We don't want that kind of scum in our town, do we, Mr. Locum?"

Locum matched his blandness. "Hell, no. But I can't tell you much. It was a camper, don't know what make. All American cars look the same to me. The color was light, maybe gray. Wait, he had a little mustache. You know, one of those waxed kind, like a foreigner."

Vogel had his notebook out. "Light-colored camper. A male Caucasian. Small mustache. Was there anybody else in the cab or in the rear?"

"Nobody I saw or heard."

"Did the man ask for any particular address on Mission Drive?"

"Just Mission Drive, that's all."

A silence. Locum looked at Vogel and then at me. "Anything else, gentlemen?"

Vogel said, "Not unless you have something more to tell us."

"Nothing, Lieutenant. See you around."

Vogel smiled. "You can make book on it."

The door closed. We walked back along the driveway to our car. Vogel was still smiling. "That man writes a better script than you or the chief. His story made sense, right?''

"Maybe to you. But *I* was there.''

We climbed into the hot car. Vogel sat quietly, staring at the big house.

I said, ''I'll give you another script, on the weird side. You remember that first day, that day we became instant buddies? You said how silly it would look for a man in a gas mask to drive Maude around town in her car.''

"That wasn't the first day. That was the second.''

"How sweet of you to remember! But how about a man in a camper? He could put her in the back and run his exhaust in there and drive around forever.''

"You might sell it to some private-eye boob-tube show,'' he said. ''But I think it's too farfetched even for that.''

I was tired and I was hot and I was angry. It was a time not to overlook an opportunity to keep my mouth shut. I kept it shut.

Along Bluff Drive, down Ridge Road, back to Main Street, in silence.

As we pulled into the police parking lot, Vogel said, ''How would he run the exhaust gases into the back?''

"By drilling a two-inch hole into the floor of the camper and running a hose through it from the tail pipe. I thought of it first, remember. The TV money is all mine.''

14

HELMS HAD SEEN US drive in; he met us in the hall. "Mrs. Gonzales," he told me, "has been waiting for over an hour. You're the only one she wants to talk with. What goes on?"

"I sent her some money through a friend," I explained. "She probably wants to thank me. Where is she?"

"In the interrogation room."

The room was small and hot. There were beads of perspiration on Mrs. Gonzales's face. She said, "Juanita gave me the money only this morning. I am with my mother now and have no need for it."

"Neither have I," I said. "Why not save it until Christmas, and buy those cute babies something extra?"

"You are a good man," she said. "Do you work here?"

"Temporarily. Why?"

She looked doubtfully around the room.

"You might have a point," I said. "It could be bugged. Why don't we go outside? That afternoon breeze is starting."

We sat on a shopper's bench, in the shade of the San Valdesto Savings and Loan building. She said, "I'm not sure I should tell this to the police. Jesus had trouble with them, and they don't forget. But Juanita said you can be trusted."

"I can be trusted. But I'm working with the police right now."

She paused for a moment, watching the traffic on the street. Then, "I'll tell you what I know. You decide how much should be private. I keep hearing how Mrs. Marner was such a wonderful woman, winning that Good Samaritan medal, and all. I don't know. . . ."

It was obvious she didn't want to go on. Prompting her might only harden the attitude. I said nothing.

"I don't know. . ." she said again.

I said, "I've learned a few things about Mrs. Marner that surprised me. Nobody's perfect, Mrs. Gonzales."

She nodded, still looking out at the street. "She and Jesus were working together on something, something they wouldn't talk to me about." Now, she looked at me. "If it was honest, why should it be secret?"

"Mrs. Marner," I explained, "was a very inquisitive woman."

She frowned. "Inquisitive? You think they were investigating something?"

"Probably. Did Jesus seem unhappy? Were you surprised when he left?"

"At first I was." Her gaze went away again. "He seemed happy. But three little children? Jesus loved parties and fun. I was seven months pregnant when he married me. I can understand now why he'd leave."

"Weren't you surprised that Lenny Tishkin would bring you the news? Jesus and Lenny were no longer friends, were they?"

"I didn't think so, not in the last year. But Lenny is the kind of man who likes to tell people bad news."

We sat there quietly for a few seconds. I asked, "Do you know a man named Otis Locum? Did Jesus ever mention him?"

She shook her head. "Never. I've never heard the name."

I stood up. "Thank you for your help. Remember, you're still young and pretty. There are a lot of good men to choose from."

"I don't need men. I have my babies. My mother will watch them during the day and I can go back to work. That welfare makes me ashamed."

Strange society we lived in. Those who couldn't learn to steal had to live in shame. I went back to the station with a troubling pattern stirring in my unconscious, some combination of incidents and attitudes that refused to emerge.

Helms and Vogel were still in Helms's office. "Well?" Vogel asked.

"Nothing important. She wanted to give me my money back. She had a feeling that her husband and Maude were involved in something illegal, but she didn't come up with a single fact."

"Who has?" Vogel said. "We got a report from San Jose that Tishkin spent a night in a motel there last week. Under his real name. That doesn't look like he's on the lam, does it?"

"Was he alone?"

"He registered as a single. Are you thinking Patty Serano?"

"I'm not thinking anything very well. Thinking isn't my strong point. I have to rely on hunches."

Vogel nodded. "I've noticed that." He rubbed his stomach. "Damn it!"

"Frustration?" I asked. "Or the gefilte fish?"

He looked at me sourly. Helms said, "The chief had his theory and nothing's come of it. What could we expect? He's administrative, not investigative.''

He's administrative, not investigative.... Gilbert and Sullivan could have made a winner out of that title if they had still been above ground. A bluebottle fly buzzed around the hot and smoky office. A siren wailed somewhere in the distance.

"We've got two facts," Helms said. "Maude's dead and there ain't nothing that will bring her back."

Vogel nodded.

I said, "Now if the chief will agree, he can issue his statement and we can drop the case."

"The only thing more obnoxious than an indignant citizen," Vogel said, "is a big-mouth indignant citizen. You and Stan Nowicki are blood brothers."

Helms smiled. "At least he puts in his time, Bernie. The man could be drinking good booze and playing bad golf now. But here he stands, sweating with us."

"No longer," I said. "See you later, gentlemen."

"Where you going?" Vogel asked.

"I'm going home. I'm not on the clock." I waited. "Unless you two have a better idea?"

"So long," Vogel said.

I went out into the hot day and into my hotter car. I opened all the windows and sat there in the police parking lot, staring through the windshield. Static contemplation; I must have caught it from Vogel.

The pattern still rumbled around in my mind. I had the uncomfortable feeling that I was overlooking the obvious. That had always been one of my strengths, recognizing the obvious.

How much time could they give it? New crimes were committed every day, new investigations started. They were understaffed and claimed to be

underpaid and the paper kept piling up at headquarters. Some wino found dead in an alley could
be written off quickly enough. Maude's promi-
nence had commanded more time, work and attention to detail.

But there were always more crimes than cops.
No investigation could go on forever. On this one
they had the convenient out—apparent suicide.

I drove down Main Street, heading for home.
Then, deciding it was still too early to go home, I
turned left on Rivera Street and parked near Kelly's Kourt.

At the far end of the court some black kids were
rolling an old tire around in a circle. At this end,
country music was coming from the open window
of the manager's mobile home.

I walked over to the angle street. It formed the
triangle with Rivera where it dead-ended at
Avalon Avenue, the minority Main Street. It
didn't actually dead-end; another street, Chapparal Road, began on the far side of Avalon and
wound its way up into the hills.

That was the road I had taken to Villwock's hermit retreat. It would be a long walk up to his place.

There were only two houses that fronted on the
street across from the vacant lot. The occupants
had been questioned; nobody had seen a car
parked there the night of the murder. That didn't
mean there hadn't been one. The residents of both
houses had been asleep long before midnight.

I came back to my car just as a gleaming new
Chevy Citation two-door came out of Kelly's
Kourt. All-American Al Pilot was on his way to
work. Either he was early or my watch was slow.
My watch read 3:44.

Jan wasn't home when I got there. I debated
with Satan for about twelve seconds, and Satan

won. I poured a big measure of bourbon into a glass and went back to all my papers.

The pattern in my unconscious had partially emerged, a pattern that traced back to what Pontius had told me. These papers wouldn't help me much with that, but I had nothing else to do. The twice-a-week gardener took care of the lawn and shrubs.

I was on Einlicher when Jan came home. "Nothing?" she asked.

"Nothing. Have a good day?"

"Not quite. Three golden hours at Phyllis Pontius's pool. Gad, that woman is dumb!"

"Her looks will carry her. Who else was there?"

"June and Julie and some woman named Norah Sullivan, a widow. She mentioned a Danning Villwock whom you're supposed to know. Do you?"

"I've met him. He's a retired parole officer. Does the widow have plans for Villwock?"

"That's the impression I got."

"Tell her to stay with the service he's probably giving her now. She'll never hook him. The man's a dedicated hermit."

Jan looked suspiciously at the Einlicher and back at me. "You've had something besides that beer. Beer never makes you malicious."

"I had a little bourbon. It's been a bad day, Jan. Don't heckle me. Please?"

She sat down next to me on the couch. She took a sip of my beer and said quietly, "Maude Marner was old and she had cancer. Her death wasn't that—that untimely, Brock."

I said nothing.

She took another sip of my beer.

"I thought the Lunds were going to Hawaii this week," I said.

"Skip canceled it. He's talking about going back to work."

"It's about time. He's only thirty-seven."

She patted my knee. "Glenys and I agree on you. You're our favorite middle-class person. I think I'll have a drink."

Her drink looked dark when she came back to the couch, almost as dark as mine had been. I said, "How about some Italian food tonight?"

"At some restaurant run by another of your girl friends?"

"Not exactly. There's a waitress there who was threatened by a Vegas hoodlum. And her daughter lived with a man for three years who might be involved in Maude's death. I can see her tomorrow if you'd rather eat at home."

She shook her head. "Whither thou goest, I will go. Your people shall be my people." She finished her drink. "But we'd better leave now. I have to go to an Auxiliary meeting at Glenys's house at eight-thirty."

The sign on the door of the Neapolitan Café informed us they were closed on Mondays.

"Where now?" I asked.

"The Biltmore," she said. "We haven't been there for ages."

Old and grand, massive and solid, the Biltmore Hotel fronted on the sea. The dining room was about half-filled. Very few of the diners were under sixty; none of them seemed to have any cosmetic urge to look younger.

At a table with a view of the beach, Paul and Phyllis Pontius were being served drinks. Paul saw us and beckoned.

"Damn it," Jan muttered. "I've already had three hours of that woman's dumb remarks! I wanted to be alone." To them, ten seconds later, she chirped, "Well, this is a pleasant surprise!"

There was room for four at the table and there were soon four. A martini for Jan, bourbon and water for me. Chitchat and persiflage. The only bright spot in the room was Phyllis, sitting across from me.

She was the subject of a few disapproving glances from time to time. These diners liked dull and quiet rooms, conditioning themselves for the grave.

We discussed the awesome accomplishment of June's county championship, the most recent gasoline shortage, and moved on to world travel, which they had experienced and we had not.

I was about halfway through my lamb stew when Phyllis said, "Skip is certainly restless lately. Have you noticed, Brock?"

"He's a young and energetic man," I explained. "It's not easy for a man like him to learn how to loaf gracefully."

"And of course," my sweet bride added, "my incurably middle-class husband has probably been needling him about his sloth."

Nothing from me except a tolerant smile.

Paul asked, "How is the investigation going, Brock?"

"Badly. I wouldn't be surprised if it's dropped soon. The file will still be open, as they call it, but the active investigation will be dropped."

"Isn't there a possibility that it actually was suicide?"

"Always. And the murderer could have banked on that."

His voice was thoughtful and quiet, maybe even troubled. "Would that indicate a professional did it?"

Was he having second thoughts about his professional friend from Vegas? I said, "Not necessarily. It could occur to any tricky amateur. There is no way of knowing how many murders are solved, because there is no way of being sure how many are committed. The percentage could be a lot worse than we might guess."

He nodded, his eyes holding mine. "I can imagine that desert around Las Vegas is studded with the graves of murdered men."

"Unsolved and unreported," I agreed. "Most of them were no loss to society. Maude was."

He nodded. "I hope they find the man, whoever he is."

We were finishing our meal when Phyllis said, "If you have anything to do tonight, Brock, Paul could drop Jan and me off at the Auxiliary meeting."

"Thank you," I said. I asked Jan, "Should I pick you up around eleven?"

She nodded. "And we can take Phyllis home."

"That would be nice," Phyllis said.

"A pleasure," I said. It would be.

I hadn't planned on doing anything. A married man's night choices were limited. I could prowl the jungle and learn nothing, as I had all day. I could go home and read, or go to a movie.

I drove along the shoreline, as close to Maude's ashes as I had been at Locum's house, depending on the ocean currents. Up Ridge Road and over the hill to town, to Padilla Street. It was possible that Moses Jones's competitive markups forced him to work nights.

He was checking the ID's of a pair of white youths who wanted a six-pack of beer when I entered his store. It was no token investigation, leading to an excuse to sell them. He questioned them sharply before he was satisfied. I had pegged him right; this man was a citizen.

They left, and he smiled at me. "What can I sell you?"

"Nothing tonight. Don't you remember me?"

"Of course. A man your size sticks in the memory. More questions?"

"Nothing specific. My wife let me out of the house tonight and I was at loose ends. Did you know Maude Marner?"

"Did I know her! She got my daughter an after-school job and she got my son a basketball scholarship at Long Beach State. He ain't built like me, that boy of mine. He got fed right. Maude bought all her wine from me."

"Is that what she drank, wine?"

"Mostly. You know what I liked about her? She was moral without being stuffy."

"My impression exactly, Mr. Jones. I have a feeling she and Jesus Gonzales might have been investigating some shenanigans down in this end of town. But you gave me a different picture of Gonzales when Vogel and I were here this morning."

"I was starting to get a better one myself, until he walked out on his wife. If they were investigating something, they didn't let me in on it."

"Do you know a girl named Patty Serano?"

He shook his head. "Am I supposed to?"

"She lived with Lenny Tishkin for about three years."

"No way I'd meet her. Lenny and I traveled in different circles."

There was still some light outside, enough for me to see the gray Maserati pulling into a parking space across the street.

"Locum," I said. "Maybe I'd better hang around awhile."

"Huh!" he said scornfully. "That big tub of lard messes with me, I'll kick his privates right through the top of his pointed head!"

"Moses," I said gently, "for a small man you're

talking awful big. I think I'd better hang around."

His smile was slightly malicious. "Inside, you mean, here in the light? Should I lock the door? If I was your size, I'd go out and belt that big pimp, just for kicks."

I smiled back at him. "Dare me."

"I dare you. I'll hold your coat."

"No need for that. I can hit pretty good with the coat on."

I went out, a Rams body directed by a junior-high-school brain, out into trouble I didn't need, stirred by an adolescent emotionalism that should have shamed me. Amateur macho, red-neck theatrics—and I was supposed to be a pro....

I was saved the trouble and the lumps. The car was empty and Otis Locum was nowhere in sight.

Moses stood on the sidewalk in front of his store. "The gutless bastard is hiding! He must have seen you heading his way."

"I doubt it," I said. "But thanks for the thought. Would you keep an ear open for me? If the police quit on this I'm going to carry on alone."

"Both ears," he promised.

15

I SAT IN MY CAR and wondered where the big man had gone. There were no houses and no stores on the other side of the street; a lumberyard and a junkyard took up the entire block. Most of the small businesses on this side of the street were closed. Only three lights were visible from where I sat. One of them was Trinity Liquors. I got out of the car to check the other two.

I could see into the first place through the display window. It was a Greek-Italian delicatessen and the only customer in the place was white and female. I couldn't see into the second place. There were dim lights on the second floor. An even dimmer light showed through the translucent glass in the upper half of the first-floor door.

A black and gilt sign below the glass identified the place:

Arden Massage Parlor
Female Staff
Private Rooms
Hours—Noon to 4:00 A.M.

Locum was probably in there, taking an order for apprentice masseuses. I went back to the car and sat. I sat for half an hour and he didn't show. And if he had? I had no authority to question him and the emotional urge to confront him was gone.

There were still two hours to fill before I was due to pick up Jan, but I had no place to go. I went home.

The people along the chief's line of inquiry who might have revealing answers were all missing—Patty Serano, Tishkin, Gonzales. I didn't have a line of inquiry, only an area. It was a doubtful area, not one I looked forward to investigating.

Phyllis Pontius wouldn't fit into the back seat of my car unless her legs were sawed off; I took Jan's car.

Through the fringe neighborhood, into the better neighborhood, through that to the best. It wasn't a bad little car, this Mercedes, both solid and responsive. The only thing really wrong with it was the price, over a hundred dollars for each cubic inch under the hood.

June was coming down the marble steps of her sister's lean-to as I came up.

"What have you done to my boy?" she asked me.

"Nothing lately. Why?"

"He thinks you disapprove of him. He's even talking about going back to work."

"There are worse sins, June."

"I guess." She stood on tiptoe to kiss my chin. "If you think it's right, it's right. You can do no wrong. I wouldn't even have the bum if it hadn't been for you."

The females were clustered in the entry hall, ready to leave. Glenys's butler waited patiently in disdainful resignation. He had come reluctantly from Beverly Hills with Glenys and never adjusted to the bucolic locals.

The women were enthused about the plans they had made at the meeting. They had decided on a dinner-dance to raise funds for the underprivileged.

They estimated a gross of ten thousand dollars. They would probably raise that much, spend ninety-nine hundred for expenses, leaving a clear hundred dollars for the underprivileged, preserving their present status.

"Why," I suggested, "don't we send those poor people a check for ten thousand dollars and then stay home and dance to some old Guy Lombardo records?"

Phyllis giggled. She appreciated my lowbrow humor.

"Don't encourage him," Jan said. "Let's go."

Only the outside front-door light and one upstairs light were visible at the Pontius mausoleum. "Thank you so much," Phyllis said. "You're very kind."

"Anytime," I said.

She looked at me quizzically and smiled. "Have a good night."

We drove past the massive homes, not visible from the road, past the large homes, partially visible, to ours.

"I wonder," Jan said, "why we haven't heard from your Aunt Sheila? Do you think she's bitter about the inheritance?"

"Not Aunt Sheila. She was always money-conscious but never money-mad. She's probably still in a honeymoon haze."

"Her fifth? Isn't that a little overromantic?"

"Not for her. I hope she's having a wonderful honeymoon. It's probably costing her plenty."

The dog from across the street who hated the *Times* let us know with a howl that he was aware of our homecoming. That started the other dogs in the neighborhood. The money spent for dog food in this long block could feed three hungry families.

"Do you remember," Jan asked, "when I lived

on Beverly Glen Boulevard and used to make you cocoa?"

"I sure do."

"Let's have some tonight."

You can't go home again, even with cocoa. Oh, world I never made, why have you become so crappy?

A CLEAR NIGHT with a light breeze, alive with moving shadows and small noises. Filled with tosses and turns, while Jan slept on, untroubled. I had no facts, no connecting links. All I had was a collection of attitudes and remarks, mostly throwaway lines, and an instinct for the obvious.

A clear night, a hot morning. The *Times* was unchewed, but the lawn was full of dog do. Someday I would buy a bull elephant with diarrhea, and let him roam the neighborhood.

Over the morning waffles, Jan asked, "Going downtown again today?"

"Yup. I don't know why, though. We were at a dead end yesterday. Maybe something happened last night."

"You mean the investigation is finished?"

"Not officially. It may never be, officially. It will simply peter out. And so will the public interest in it."

"You sound cynical, hubby."

"I've been working with cynical men. No, that's not fair. I've been working with—with realists."

Something had happened last night. Lenny Tishkin had been picked up in Morro Bay.

In the hall, Vogel told me, "Helms went up to get him." He paused. "So what do we hold him on?"

"An old pro like you should be able to think of something. How about suspicion of robbery?"

"He's already been acquitted of that."

"Of Trinity Liquors. But not A-1 Beverages or the Padilla Grog Shop."

"Neither Leeds nor Adler will testify. You heard 'em say so."

"Suspicion of murder?"

"Whose? We've learned that Tishkin was in Oakland on the night Maude died."

"Bernie," I said, "your voice is shaking. Easy, man."

"Easy, hell! The chief screams about bad police work. I say he's wasting the taxpayers' money, running down Tishkin."

"Cool it, Loot. The man can be held for questioning about Gonzales's disappearance. Maybe he's got a habit. If he's held long enough without a fix, he could loosen up."

"He's got no habit," Vogel said coldly. "And Farini's been phoning about him already."

"Joe Farini? How did he find out about it? I thought Nowicki was Tishkin's lawyer."

"So did I. But Tishkin phoned Farini from Morro Bay as soon as he was grabbed. The punk's gone big time."

"Or maybe Locum's picking up the tab. Why don't we talk to Leeds and Adler again? They might change their minds."

"I've already talked with both of them on the phone," he said bitterly, "and they both laughed at me."

I smiled. "So it isn't the taxpayers' money that's got you riled. It's the taxpayers' scorn."

"Shut up. Amateurs and politicians, that's what I get to work with!"

"Bernie," I said soothingly, "let's not make this the shortest friendship on record. I'm on your side, man!"

His voice was quieter. "I'm sorry, Brock. I guess I need a vacation. You've been—" He stopped and stared past me. "Oh, Christ, here he comes now."

Big Joe Farini was coming down the hall. I had met him when he had represented Skip.

"Well, Mr. Callahan," he said genially, "we meet again. Only this time, I see, you're working *with* the police."

"It's more fun this way," I said. "You should try it, counselor."

His smile faded. "Watch your tongue, footballer. You're not that big."

"There's a way to find out," I said.

From a smile to a stare and now to a glare. "Are you threatening me?"

I nodded.

He looked at Vogel. "You heard that, Lieutenant. You might be called as a witness."

"My hearing aid was turned off," Vogel said wearily. "What do you want, Joe?"

"I want to know when Tishkin is due here. All I get from that sergeant at the desk is static."

"He'll be here as soon as Helms gets him here. Sergeant Helms is a slow driver. We'll let you know."

"Immediately," Farini said.

"If he gets here immediately, we'll inform you immediately. If he doesn't, we'll inform you when he does get here. Anything else?"

Farini looked between us speculatively—and made the wise decision. "Nothing," he said. "Thank you." He went back down the hall.

Vogel shook his head. "With your mouth, you sure need your size."

"It helps. Come on, I'll buy you a cup of coffee."

He hadn't had his breakfast, so I bought him more than coffee, an Egg McMuffin and a side order of French fries. I helped him with the fries.

We came back to the police parking lot the same time as Helms arrived. No department car had been available last night. Helms used his own and would get mileage added to his overtime credit.

My mental picture of Lenny Tishkin had been awry. He stood on the blacktop of the parking lot, neatly dressed in fawn slacks and a light yellow sport shirt, a slim young man with curly chestnut hair and big brown eyes. He could have been an Eagle scout.

Lenny stayed where he was while Helms came over to us. "He's changed his story a little. The way he tells it now, he didn't go to the bus station with Gonzales. He happened to be there when Gonzales left town."

"What was he doing at the bus station?" Vogel asked.

"Waiting for a friend from out of town—he claims."

"A friend we can check?"

Helms smiled. "I'll give you one guess."

"Sure," Vogel said. "Natch! You'd better phone Farini. He's been on my neck all morning. I'll take Tishkin in."

The chief wanted to see him, too, so we gathered in his office, Tishkin, Farini, Helms, Vogel and yours truly, citizen observer.

Chief Chandler Harris sat behind his desk, studying some papers, molding his face into the Santa Claus image. Finally, he looked up and smiled at the lad he had called a vicious punk who had learned to lie when he had learned to talk.

"Well, Lenny, it's certainly comforting to see you on our side of the street, for a change."

Farini frowned. Lenny smiled.

"You heard about the death of your good friend, I suppose?" Harris went on. "Mrs. Marner?"

Lenny nodded. "I read about it in the Oakland paper."

"You didn't come down for her memorial service. At least, I didn't see you there."

"I wasn't there," Lenny said.

"Fine lady," Harris said. "As I remember, she arranged to get Stanley Nowicki to defend you on the robbery charge. Young Nowicki is probably the best defense attorney in town."

"Easy, Chief," Farini said.

Harris smiled. "Nothing personal, Joe. We've known each other a long time." He frowned. "Maybe too long?"

Farini said coolly, "I have advised my client to be cooperative. But I don't like the trend of this meeting."

The Santa Claus image had melted in the hot room. Harris's face was a mask. "I intend to ask your client about a certain discrepancy in a story he told. Would you like to consult with him first?"

"Information he gave to a police officer?"

Harris shook his head.

Farini looked at Tishkin. Tishkin said, "I know what he's talking about. It's easily explained. I told Maria Gonzales I had gone to the bus station with Jesus. I lied. Jesus and I weren't close, anymore, but I didn't think Maria knew that. I was. . . ." He paused. "Well, I guess I was trying to comfort her. I always liked Maria."

"Couldn't you have explained to her you were waiting at the station for a friend from out of town?"

Tishkin nodded. "I should have. I guess I wasn't thinking straight. I mean, though, there was Maria with those three babies, and Jesus just taking off like that. I wanted her to think of me as a friend, I guess.''

Clean, innocent, cooperative young man with curly hair and those big brown eyes.... He had moved up a rung on the larceny ladder, from stick-ups to the big con. He no longer needed a public defender; what cop would roust this young, short-haired, establishment citizen?

The words went back and forth in the room, meaning nothing, leading nowhere. We couldn't hold the punk, but as a favor to us he promised to stay around town for a few days. He had brought enough fresh clothes.

If you wonder why cops are cynical and inclined to carry short fuses, you should meet the citizens they have to deal with—on both sides of the law.

Harris finished his questioning and looked around the room. ''Anybody else?''

Vogel said, ''That's a fancy motel you were staying at up in Morro Bay, Lenny. Are you working now?''

Farini started to protest, but Tishkin silenced him with a gesture. ''I'm working,'' he said. ''I'm selling mutual funds.''

Vogel smiled and shook his head. ''I have no other questions.''

We all went out, except for the chief. In the hall Farini said, ''No hard feelings, I hope, Mr. Callahan. I guess we got off to a bad start. Give Miss Christopher my regards when you see her.''

''I'll tell her how it was,'' I promised. ''And I'll tell the Lunds, too. But don't blame me. They were thinking of changing lawyers anyway.''

16

In Helms's office, Vogel asked, "Wasn't it Joe Farini who defended Lund in that mess he was in?"

"Right. He was mostly a criminal lawyer then. But Skip was grateful, and he introduced him to his rich friends. Now Farini has reverted, the way it looks. Why, I wonder?"

"Maybe the hoodlum rich pay better. That old-money crowd aren't too generous with their help." He smiled. "That was a stiff shot you gave him in the hall. Below the belt, maybe, but I enjoyed it."

"That's the only place you can hurt lawyers," I said, "in the wallet. So what have we learned that we didn't know?"

"Nothing," Helms said. "About the only good that came out of the trip was the dough I'll pick up on mileage. I've got to talk to the Optimists this noon. I'd better get cleaned up and shaved. See you later, boys."

"And I've got to be in court at two o'clock," Vogel said. "Any place we can go before then, citizen?"

"None I can think of."

"Well," he said, "I've got two acres of paperwork long overdue. This might be the time for it. If you get any bright ideas, holler." He waved and left the room.

He had suckered me out of seven bucks. I had paid off our bet too soon. When had *any* police department officially announced that the investigation of a murder was no longer active?

Who needed them? That's what I asked myself, standing on the cracked blacktop of the parking lot in the hot sun, wondering where to go next.

Almost six and a half days, a lot of man-hours, had been spent by the department on the mysterious death of Maude Marner. Helms had to carry on with his public relations, Vogel had to catch up with his reports. The still living public needed protection. What else could I have expected?

I, too, could go back to my regular routine—but it was ladies' day at the club. This patchwork theory, constructed of bits and pieces, kept floating around in my brain.

Tishkin had been no help. Gonzales, I was beginning to believe, might never be located. There had been no strenuous department effort to find Patty Serano. To the department, she had been only a bystander.

Lenny had lived with her for almost three years. Among today's young people, three years was a long stretch of loyalty. He must have found some meaning in the relationship, as they phrase it.

I went back to the middle-class street where the waitress lived. Her Cadillac was in the driveway, a Camaro was visible through the open garage door.

Mary didn't open the door to my ring. Al Pilot's spiritual twin stood there, a broad, big-bellied man in a T-shirt, wearing a scowl.

"What are you selling?" he asked me.

"Nothing, sir," I said. "Are you Mr. Serano?"

"That's right."

"Could I speak with your wife?"

"Why?"

"It's about your daughter, sir, your daughter Patty."

"My daughter is dead. She's been dead for two years."

He stared at me. I stared back.

And then, from behind him, his wife said, "What the hell's going on, Pete? What did you say about Patty?"

"You heard me," he said, "and so did he. Goodbye, mister."

His wife edged past him. "Mr. Callahan! Come in, come in."

"Maybe you had better vote on it." I suggested. "I'm not looking for trouble."

"Don't worry about him," she said. "He's all mouth and belly. Come on in." She turned to her husband. "Go suck up another beer and stay out of sight. Don't we already have enough problems with the neighbors?"

He went into the kitchen. We went into the living room. "Have you news about Patty?" she asked me.

I shook my head. "I thought you might. It's possible she could have some information I need."

"Find Lenny Tishkin," she said, "and you'll find Patty."

"Lenny was picked up by the police last night in Morro Bay, and brought back here for questioning," I told her. "He was alone. Do you think Patty's in town?"

"I have no idea. Thank God she wasn't with Lenny when he was picked up. I haven't heard from her in six months. My husband's disowned her, but—" She gestured toward a chair. "I'm sorry. Won't you sit down? Would you like something cool to drink?"

"No, thanks." I sat on the chair, she on a love

seat nearby. I asked, "She and Lenny were very close for a while, weren't they?"

"Nobody can get close to Lenny Tishkin," she said. "What was he going to be questioned about?"

"About the disappearance of a young man named Jesus Gonzales. Did Patty know him?"

"If she did, she never mentioned him to me. You're the man who found out about that bastard who threatened me, aren't you?"

"Yes. I guess it was just a joke. A bad one, but a joke."

"Mobsters don't joke," she said. "That's what he was, wasn't he?"

"Probably. Mrs. Serano, my only interest in Patty is information she might have. My only interest in this investigation is finding the murderer of Maude Marner. I seem to be working alone on it right now, and I don't have any official credentials, so I could certainly use friends who could help."

"You're not working with the police anymore?"

"With them, but not for them."

She looked past me, her face thoughtful. "I might be able to help. I—have friends who might know something." She met my gaze. "But I want a promise from you."

"Name it."

Her voice was low, too low to be heard in the kitchen. "If you find Patty, I want you to let me know. No matter what she's doing, or where she's doing it, I want to know. Do you understand me?"

"Clearly. I worked on a few cases in Los Angeles where I had to lie to parents."

"Not to me you don't. My life hasn't been that sheltered."

"I'll do what I can," I promised. "But remember, I'm working alone."

"Not anymore you aren't."

"Do you have a picture of her?"

She shook her head. "My husband burned them all. Maybe I can get a picture from the high-school yearbook from one of her friends. I'll try."

When I went out, her husband was standing in the driveway in his sweat-stained T-shirt, with a can of beer in his hand, visible to all the neighbors.

Where now? Juanita? Moses Jones? Neither had phoned me, but I headed for their neighborhood.

I was pulling into a parking space in front of Trinity Liquors when I saw Lenny Tishkin. He was coming out of a doorway up the block a ways.

I walked up the street to the doorway, and it was what I expected, the Arden Parlor. I pushed open the door.

Directly ahead were the steps to the second floor. On my left, an archway revealed a small office. The only occupant of the office was a woman of about fifty. Her stout body was encased in a clean, white nurse's uniform, but her eyes were the blasé eyes of an old hooker.

She was sitting behind a desk and facing the archway. "Yes, sir?" she said, smiling her mechanical smile.

I made my smile embarrassed. "I was in town some time ago, visiting my brother. I had this muscle pull in my thigh and you certainly helped it. There was an operator named—Patty?"

"Patty Serano," she said. "This is a coincidence! Another of her good friends was just in asking about her. Unfortunately, Patty went down to Los Angeles last week. But don't you worry, sir. All of our operators are highly skilled." She smirked. "And as pretty as Patty."

I looked doubtful. "Gosh, I don't know. She was

sure great. Won't she be back? I'll be in town for quite a while.''

"I think she might be back soon," the old girl said, "now that her other friend is back in town. I could phone you, if you'll be in town for a while."

"For at least a month," I told her. "My brother lives up on Bluff Drive, but I don't know his telephone number."

"I'm sure it's in the book," she said with brassy sweetness. "Your name, sir?"

"Sydney," I said. "Sydney Locum. My brother's name is Otis."

The smile went away and the granite eyes turned to chrome. She glared at me as I smiled at her. Her voice was harsh. "What's your pitch, buster?"

"Just checking your connections," I said. "Hang in there, chubby!" I waved and went out.

Moses wasn't in his place. A tall, thin youth, tall enough to play basketball for Long Beach State, was behind the counter, ringing up a sale. I climbed into the hot car and headed for the dim coolness of Chickie's.

Juanita was working the bar. The lunch trade wasn't big here; she wasn't needed in the kitchen. Her smile had some trepidation in it. She gestured toward the Einlicher spigot.

"In a minute," I said. "I have to make a call."

I looked up the number and used the wall phone. Mrs. Serano answered.

I told her, "I learned a few minutes ago that Patty went down to Los Angeles about a week ago."

"Where did you learn that?"

She could take the truth, she had assured me. But I couldn't deliver it. "From a friend," I said. "From a reliable source. This source thinks that Patty will come back here if she learns Lenny is in town."

"Oh, God—well, thank you. We have relatives down there and maybe she'll look one of them up. I'll be in touch with you, Mr. Callahan, on the other matter."

Juanita had a beaker of beer ready when I reached the bar. Her smile was doubtful. "Friends, Pancho?"

"Why not? We all have to make a living. There are some friends I've had to protect from the police, too."

"I could tell you a *few* things."

"At lunch. I'm hungry. What's good besides enchiladas?"

"I have gringo food. A nice little steak, on toast, and maybe a salad?"

I nodded.

"You're blue," she said. "I have made you blue."

I shook my head.

She smiled again. "You know who dropped in for the first time in years this morning? Skip! It was so good to see him once more."

"I guess he's getting reorganized. He might even go back to work."

"I hope so. He's a handsome devil, isn't he?"

"I never noticed."

She gave my order to the waitress and came with me to our little corner table. She had brought a glass of beer along. She sipped it and wiped her mouth and looked at me.

"For the last month," she told me, "the people who pay off in this town pay it to Otis Locum. If they don't, things happen to them."

"And before last month?"

She shook her head.

"To one of your friends?"

She shrugged.

"That's one thing. You promised me a few."

"Two more. A man named Leonard Tishkin gets girls for Locum. A man named Barney Leeds, who runs a liquor store, he also books and he pays Locum."

I said, "I'm getting the feeling that everybody in this is your friend—except Otis Locum."

Her face stiffened.

"A little joke," I explained.

"Sometimes, Pancho, your jokes are not funny."

The waitress brought my steak and salad and a bowl of soup for Juanita. Silence, while we ate, silence between friends. As I had told her before, we all have to make a living. Who was I to judge her? Some of the angles I'd had to work to survive in Los Angeles. . . .

I asked, "Does Otis give them protection, too?"

"A lawyer," she said. "Joe Farini, usually. And bail money."

"Do you know Mary Serano?"

She nodded.

"Does she pay off, too?"

"Never before, not Mary. But the word I get, she may have to, now."

"I wonder why not before?"

"I could guess. There are more Chicanos down here than there are blacks. We all like Mary, even if she is Italian."

"You mean you have a Mexican Mafia?"

"Damn you! What kind of talk is that?"

"Sour talk," I said. "Bitter talk. I apologize."

"You're a strange man," she said. "Rich now, with a lovely wife, but you can't keep your nose out of the dirt, can you?"

"I guess not. Juanita, we're still friends, but we live in a complicated world."

"Whatever that means. Kiss me, friend."

I stood up and came over to kiss her. I said, "Chin up! Both of us are better off than Maude Marner."

She said nothing. I put some bills on the table and went out into the sun. Where now? Where else? The Padilla Grog Shop.

Barney Leeds was sitting in a captain's chair near his display window, reading *The Racing Form.* He was a tall, fairly thin man, except for the belt-line bulge.

He looked up and asked, "Where's your partner?"

"Catching up on his paperwork. I have only one question. Before Otis Locum came into the picture, who collected from you?"

He stared at me. "You're not making sense. Collected what? I charge the regular retail markup. I don't have to pay off anybody."

"I'm not talking about your booze. I'm talking about your book."

"Get lost!" he said. "What are you trying to pull?"

"I was hoping for the truth. Don't keep too much cash in your register. Tishkin's back in town."

"Beat it!" he said. "If you want to play cop, get yourself a badge."

He wasn't very heavy. I could easily have thrown him through his front window. Some other violent alternatives ran through my mind—before I went quietly out.

17

I WAS MAKING MORE ENEMIES than headway. The course should be open by now; even on ladies' day the ladies were restricted to playing in the morning. Nobody was paying me and very few people seemed to care whether or not Maude Marner's killer was ever brought to justice.

Untrue, Callahan, and you know it. There are people who care, but they don't move in your circles.

Vogel would now be in court and Helms would still be laughing (and lapping) it up with the cheerful Optimists. I climbed into my clunker and drove down to the sea.

I sat on a bench and looked out at the gray, dull Pacific, the decaying kelp on the sand, the strollers and the surfers, the big-bosomed girls in their bikinis.

Locum was the obvious target. But I couldn't believe he was a complicated man. If he planned to kill somebody, he wouldn't gimmick it. Above (or behind) Locum, who was there? Somebody with money or somebody with clout, somebody who could read the public mind, who had met the citizens at all economic levels and sensed their apathy.

I went back to the station at three-thirty. Neither Helms nor Vogel was there. Vogel was still in court. Helms was on an emergency call; there had been a racial disturbance out at the university.

I came home to a strange sight, Jan practicing chip shots on the front lawn. A golfing wife? Dear God, haven't I suffered enough?

She was not alone. Skip Lund was her instructor.

"You're starting wrong," I told her. "Your teacher is known as Shank-Shot Lund."

"The second worst in the club," he admitted. "How's it going, Sherlock?"

"Badly. I have an uneasy feeling that the department is losing interest. I hear you've been looking up your old friends."

"A few of them. When I hung around down there, I got to know some shady characters. I thought they might tell me things they wouldn't tell you or Vogel."

I said nothing, nonplussed.

"He wants to help," Jan explained. "That's why he's here. He was waiting for you."

"Knowing your jealous disposition," Skip added, "we waited outside."

"We can go in now and discuss it over some bourbon. I've gone through a hot, bad day on one beer." I looked at Jan for approval.

"Get stoned, for all I care," she said. "I'm going to stay out here and practice."

In the den, I told Skip, "Thanks for nothing. You could have done me less damage in the bedroom. That's all I need in the family, a lady golfer."

"Every man has his own cross, muscles. It makes more sense than tennis. I'll have Scotch over ice."

I poured him a jolt heavy enough to loosen his tongue and matched it in good American corn for me.

We sat in the barrel chairs and he asked musingly, "Did you and Juanita ever—"

"Never," I interrupted. "Let's get to the business at hand. Did you learn anything today?"

"Nothing."

"I thought she might tell you something she wouldn't tell me."

"No. You were always her favorite. Some of the men I knew down there are now in jail. The few I talked with today could have resented my tailoring. Tomorrow, I'll dress in the old image."

I said nothing.

"You're laughing at me, aren't you? Inside."

"I am not. You know those people better than I do. When did you decide to play Hawkshaw?"

"After your Sunday-morning sermon. I don't plan it as a trade. But I knew people down there who could still be there, people who won't talk to any cop, public or private."

"Which means you won't be traveling with me."

"Wouldn't it be better if we each went our own route?"

"Probably. My credentials are shaky enough. You don't have any."

"I'm a citizen," he said. "There's no law I know of against a citizen asking questions."

"Not yet. Maybe soon. Another jolt?"

He nodded. "Then I can go home and hear about serves and lobs and volleys. It's not easy to listen to, sober."

Jan was still practicing when he left. She shanked some and topped others, but in her second hour of golf she had already surpassed me in chipping.

"You could buy me a set of clubs for our anniversary," she suggested. "I think this old set of yours is too heavy for me."

"Our anniversary is March fourteenth."

"Our five months' anniversary," she explained. "Tomorrow."

I changed the subject. "What's for dinner?"

"Meat loaf, cruel master. I won't be home tonight. We have to make out the invitation list for the dance."

Plebeian food, meat loaf, geared to my palate. I wolfed it down, along with the scalloped potatoes and the broccoli.

And then Jan went to the Lunds' to help work out the pattern of selective snobbery and I was left with nobody but the neighbors' dogs, sniffing around our front lawn, hunting for a plant they might have left unkilled.

I was about to turn on Walter Cronkite when the phone rang.

It was Moses Jones. "I just now figured out where that Locum must have disappeared to, last night."

"So have I. The Arden Massage Parlor. I was in there today, asking questions. Don't get me wrong; I didn't go upstairs."

"Did you notice something kooky when you were in there?"

I thought about it for a few seconds. "Well, there was only a narrow office downstairs, and a narrow hall. There was no door leading off the hall or the office. The upstairs must be wider than the downstairs, isn't it?"

"Nope. How could it be? The outside to the rest of the downstairs is off the alley in back. There's a parking lot there, too. A friend of mine told me about it today. Three poker tables and a crap table."

"Locum's?"

"Sure is."

"Maybe I'll drop in for a little poker tonight."

"Nothin' personal, but you might not be welcome."

"Moses," I informed him sadly, "nobody in the world is more welcome at a poker table than I am."

"Okay. You need a tough backup man, I could close the store."

"That wouldn't be fair," I said. "We don't want to overwhelm them. But thanks for the offer. Keep in touch."

"Right on!"

They wouldn't be starting this early. Walter Cronkite explained how the world was moving, how it had been this day of our lives. "The Gong Show" followed. In prime time!

I went out to spray the shrubs with dog repellent. I should have sprayed the picture tube.

The sun sank lower. I put on one of the pre-inheritance suits I had saved for sentimental reasons, a snappy number from Discount Danny's. I had about a hundred in my wallet and Jan had stashed fifty dollars in her handkerchief box. Even with my inconsiderable skills, that should last through a two-dollar game—if I played them tight.

It was dark now. I took the freeway to the Padilla turnoff, through heavy traffic. The alley didn't open off Padilla, but I finally found it.

The parking lot was on the other side of the building, at the rear of a furniture store. Among the parked cars were a gray Maserati and a red Porsche. Skip drove a red Porsche. So did a score of other local citizens.

A dim light shone over a weathered door. On the

door was a sign: Arden Community Club—Members Only.

The door was locked. There was a bell button next to it, which I pushed. From somewhere in the dark above the light, a public address speaker asked, "Number, please?"

"I don't have a number," I said. "My name is Callahan, and I brought cash."

"All our members have numbers."

"I'm not a member. I have some credit cards, if you want to check me out."

A pause, a silence, and the door opened partway. A short but very muscular black man stood there, wearing a gaudy sport shirt and gaudier slacks. "You come to see Mr. Locum?"

"I didn't even know he was here. I came to play poker."

He opened the door wider. "Okay. Come in."

The lights in the room were hanging lights, one over each poker table, one over the dice table. A dice game was going on and two poker games. Most of the men at the crap table were black, the men at the poker tables were either black or Chicano. There was only one other Anglo face in the room, Skip Lund's. He was playing poker.

He didn't see me. Otis Locum stood next to the small bar in the nearest corner. "The honky peeper," he said. "You come here for trouble or for action?"

From all around the room, faces swiveled our way. Locum's gaze measured them. He must have realized they couldn't all be friendly. Their fear of him was probably the only reason many of them were subservient. I had to bank on that.

I kept my voice calm. "Let's make a deal. If you don't call me a honky peeper, I won't call you a penny-ante pimp."

The volcano erupted. Locum came at me with a roar.

If he had come at me, a man his size, fists clenched in the honorable American macho tradition, fist against fist, pound for pound, I would have been forced to honor the tradition. But he brought a bottle from the bar with him.

What he didn't know, of course, was that I had been the punter with the Rams during my first two seasons. He had the bottle raised—when I put my size-twelve brogan squarely into the middle of his jewel box.

He doubled, groaning, and I brought my knee up into the middle of his face. I could feel his front teeth crack, along with the cartilage in his nose, before he crashed to the floor.

Some scrawny, long-haired man clawed at me from one side, while the bouncer in the gaudy shirt circled behind. I threw the scrawny man into the bouncer and backed up to the crap table, eliminating any sneak attacks from the rear.

Skip was next to me now, the two of us the only Anglos in the room. What I had hoped for, what I had banked on, was that this would not evolve into an ethnic war.

There had to be, in that room, some men who resented the dominance of Otis Locum. There had to be some who recognized that this was the good guys against the bad guys and they were good guys. And then, there had to be some of my spiritual brothers.

I mean the two-dollar horseplayers. The poker players, like yours truly, who draw to inside straights and raise before the draw on four hearts. Maybe this would shape up as the losers against the winners. There were warriors already lined up with Skip and me against the crap table.

But it couldn't have been the winners against the losers, because we all know there are more losers than winners in this world, and we were sadly outnumbered.

We never would have won it. But we lasted long enough to remain vertical until the men in blue arrived to end the hostilities.

18

CAPTAIN DAHL was in charge of the night watch. I knew him; Skip knew him better. All the others had gone home on bail. Locum was in the hospital. Skip and I sat with Captain Dahl in the interrogation room. Skip had a fat lip and a bruised eye; all my damage had been to my stomach. Breathing was painful.

"Disturbing the peace or inciting to riot," Dahl said. "I don't know how to book you."

Skip grinned. "Why not call it a citizen's arrest? You boys won't raid the joint. Somebody has to."

"Very funny, Lund. What do you two call yourselves, the Montevista Vigilantes?"

Skip shook his head. "Concerned citizens. You and Linda still making music, Captain?"

Dahl's voice was ice. "Be very careful, Warren Temple Lund. Your wife's money doesn't buy you anything here."

Skip started to come out of his chair, but I pushed him back. I said, "Captain, it was all my fault. And let's put this into perspective. Who was hurt?"

"Otis Locum. Four teeth gone, a broken nose, possible internal injuries. That's the latest word from the hospital."

"He came at me with a bottle. If he hadn't he might have stayed out of the hospital. Has he filed a complaint?"

Dahl didn't answer.

"He refused to," I guessed.

"So far," Dahl admitted. "What difference does it make? For a week now, Callahan, you've been working under department sanction. How does this make us look?"

"Who's looking? There isn't a reporter around, and there hasn't been one."

Dahl's gaze swiveled between us, back and forth.

Skip said quietly, "I apologize for my remark, Captain."

Dahl studied him for a few seconds. Then, "All right. I apologize, too. I'll let the chief decide this one tomorrow. Get out of here, both of you."

In the hallway, Skip said, "I wonder who called the law?"

"A man named Moses Jones. He told me he had, after the wagon came. I gave him my keys. His son is watching your car. Who is that Linda you were bugging Dahl about?"

"A girl I knew. A girl a lot of men knew. The captain's been living with her for four years. I hear they plan to get married soon."

"That was a real cheap shot, Skip."

"I know. I don't like cops. Who should know the reason why better than you?"

"Someday, when you're thinking straight, try to imagine what the world would be without them."

"So, all right, already, I did wrong. Where the hell's that Detroit junker of yours?"

"Waiting on the lot with my chauffeur."

Moses came out of the darkness into the reflected light from a station window. "Where's Locum? I didn't see him come out."

"He's in the hospital," I said. "Guess who put him there."

"You. Didn't I tell you you could take that slob?"

I introduced him to Skip and he held the car door open for both of us. He evidently planned to act as our chauffeur.

"I'll drive," I told him. "This is a high-performance machine."

"I sure didn't notice that." He climbed into the back seat.

His son was waiting on the lot behind the Arden Community Club. He was sitting in Skip's Porsche, six feet and nine inches of young man with a future. Even if he hadn't been tall, I was sure any son of Moses Jones would have a future worth having.

Back to the Padilla ramp, back to the freeway. There had been a savage joy in me when I smashed Locum's face. There was a rising of nausea in me now, the same nausea I had felt when I broke Josh Leddy's leg on that cold afternoon in Green Bay when we creamed the Packers.

There had been no joy in the Leddy collision. Josh Leddy was white. Did that make me a racist? I thought of all those young runaway girls Otis Locum had sold into bondage. I reminded myself that black Moses Jones hated him as much as I did. But the nausea kept rising.

It was two o'clock, but Jan was still up, waiting for me. Skip had phoned June before Jan left their house, so she knew about what had happened.

"You finally had your fight with Otis Locum," she said. "Is that why you went down there?"

I shook my head. "I didn't even know he'd be there. Is there any Alka Seltzer in the house?"

"You've been drinking!"

I didn't stop to argue. I barely had time to make the nearest growler. It all came up, meat loaf, broccoli, scalloped potatoes and bile. A great sense of marital injustice replaced it in my gut. You've been drinking. . . .

She was waiting outside the bathroom door. "I'm sorry."

"You should be. I haven't had a drink since before dinner. But I took a lot of shots to the belly and I'm not proud of what I did to Locum. Would you make some tea?"

Tea, a return to suburban quiet, a domestic report of the night's adventure, starting with Moses' phone call.

"I had it wrong," Jan said. "I thought you and Skip had gone down there together, looking for trouble."

"You had it wrong," I agreed. "Be sure all the doors are locked. Locum didn't file a complaint with the police. He has his own law."

In the warm, dim, cozy breakfast room, she stared at me. "You don't think—he wouldn't—"

"I don't know what he will do. I am hoping to put him away before he decides to take any action. I'm not sure the department will cooperate, not after tonight."

"They'd better! I'll have Glenys make some phone calls."

Sure. Write to the bureaucrats, phone them, get back a form letter. No wonder the kids had resorted to rioting. What other route was there?

THE MORNING was overcast and cool. The *Times* was unchewed; the repellent seemed to have worked, though I hadn't bothered to take a count last night.

Pork sausages, eggs, toast and coffee restored my sanity.

"How's your stomach?" Jan asked. She looked

at my empty plate. "I withdraw the question. You really are tough, aren't you?"

I shrugged modestly. "I have to think of something to tell the chief. He has a tendency to make impulsive decisions."

"You could kick him in the groin," she suggested.

She was trying to be the white, female Moses Jones. A noble effort, earning her a kiss, which I gave her.

"By the way," I said, "I kissed Juanita yesterday. Only because she asked me to. There were others present."

"Let her keep her kisses," my bride said, "and come up with some facts. She failed you, Brock."

Hell hath no fury like a noncombatant. "Give her time," I said. "Faith, kid. She has to live down there."

Vogel was in the chief's office when I got to the station. So was Skip. Vogel was grinning. "It had to happen. It was overdue."

The chief wasn't grinning. "What exactly did you mean by that, Lieutenant?"

Vogel looked at his superior with the composure of a man sure of his pension and his skill at power. "Locum's been asking for it. He's been insolent to every officer who ever questioned him. He's been harassing Mr. Callahan. A few nights ago he threatened him. I'm sure, sir, the department shouldn't have any confusion about which man to support in a Callahan-Locum confrontation."

Harris studied him wearily. "Maybe I'd better send *you* out on the lecture circuit and switch Helms to traffic."

"I was on the debating team at college, sir."

The chief's face grew rosier. "Easy, Lieutenant. Don't overplay your hand."

Vogel smiled. "Not with you, Chief. It cost me eighteen dollars one night."

Harris's voice was calmer. "You got all the right words ready for Farini, too?"

"Has he called?"

"Not yet."

"Would you like to wager my eighteen dollars that we won't hear a peep out of that shyster?"

"All right, all right!" He looked at Lund. "You were gambling there, weren't you, playing poker for money?"

"Penny-ante stuff," Skip said. "There were no eighteen-dollar bets at *that* table."

The chief looked us over, one man at a time. Then, "It's too damned early in the day for bad comedy. You can all leave if you leave quickly. Go!"

In Vogel's office, Skip asked, "Could we be friends, Lieutenant?"

Vogel smiled. "Any friend of Callahan's is half-way there." He held out a hand.

I asked, "Are we working today?"

"Today," he told me, "we're setting up a city-wide narcotics bust. We'll need every officer we can lay our hands on, including Helms."

Vogel picked up the phone and began to dial. I waved a goodbye and went out with Skip. The overcast was leaving, the temperature rising.

I asked Skip, "Still plan to go your own way?"

He nodded. "You've been seen around town with Vogel all week. That means fuzz to my former friends." He grinned. "And you know something, Brock? Even though you're not one, you look like a cop."

"Thank you. Phone me tonight if you learn anything."

The man from Vegas had been a red herring. At

least, that's the way he was cast in my revision of
the chief's script. I had promised to alert Pontius if
I checked the man, but I decided the information
Villwock had given me made the promise inopera-
tive.

The Dolor Clinic was directly across the street
from Valley Hospital, in the western section of
town. I knew the director, a high-handicapper
named Malcolm Prescott. That could be an entry,
but I wasn't sure how far the inviolate doctor-
patient relationship extended.

Prescott was in his office, due right now, he informed me, at a staff meeting.

"A man from Nevada?" he said, frowning.
"Around the eighth or ninth of this month?" He
looked at me doubtfully.

"I'm working with the police," I told him in a
dignified and (I hoped) authoritative voice. "This
information could help us find the man who murdered Si Marner's mother."

He glanced at his wristwatch and frowned some
more. "Nevada, you say? Las Vegas, I suppose. We
get a lot of them."

"Maybe not that week."

He sighed. "Okay. I have to leave. I'll tell Vickie
to help you."

Vickie was a well-shaped brunette in a well-
fitted uniform, wearing Jan's fragrance, Norell.

She riffled through some file cards and said,
"Francis Martin, Las Vegas, August ninth. He's
the only one that week." She shook her head and
smiled. "He's moved up in the world and changed
his name."

"You know the man?"

"I went to high school with him. He was Frank
Martino then. Sexy little Italian. He had a Mafia
uncle he used to boast about."

"Do his folks still live in town?"

"No. They moved to one of those retirement horrors down there near San Diego. Nice people. Very active in the P.T.A."

"Which high school was that?"

"The only one we had then, San Valdesto."

"I don't want to be indelicate, but how long ago was that?"

"I graduated in 1961," she said demurely. "I look younger, though, don't I?"

"I judged you to be no more than twenty-six," I assured her. "Thanks, Vickie."

I stood in front of the clinic, in the emerging sun, and stared across the street at the Valley Hospital. I went over, finally, planning to ask for Otis Locum's room number. Not that I wanted to visit him, only to make sure he was still there, and not prowling the tree-shaded lanes of Montevista.

I didn't need to inquire; I almost bumped into Joe Farini in the lobby.

He backed off and glared at me. "If you plan to question my client, I intend to go up with you. You'll be hearing from us, eventually, about last night's attack."

"Don't threaten me, Joe. You're even smaller than he is. Why don't you go down to the station bullpen and rustle up some new clients?"

He glared and glared—and walked away.

I waited until he was out of sight before going back to my car. A remark of Mary Serano's stirred in my memory, that remark about her daughter's picture in the high-school annual. I headed for the school.

The vice-principal, a man named Alger Luplow, was in charge of the summer session. His body followed the same general penguin contours as Chief Chandler Harris's, but his face was kinder.

"That's an interesting concept," he agreed. "San Valdesto graduates of the sixties and what they're doing today. Are you a writer, Mr. Callahan?"

"I'm working on a script," I admitted. "I'm not sure it will sell."

"Persistence," he told me gently, "is the writer's strongest ally. We have a full file of annuals in the school library. Mrs. Vogel, our summer-session librarian, will be only too happy to help you."

"I can't win any," Vogel had said. "My wife is a part-time librarian."

She was a trim, slim little woman, a Maude Marner thirty years younger. "Mr. Callahan!" she greeted me. "We finally meet. Bernie has told me so much about you. Is he with you?"

"He's deserted me today," I said. "What's this business about graduates of the sixties? Mr. Luplow wasn't very clear about it."

"It was a little fantasy I told him to brighten his day. What I'm really looking for is a picture of a man named Frank Martino. He graduated in the early sixties."

"I wasn't here then," she said. "I was up in Berkeley, trying to get my hooks into Bernie." She led me to the section where the annuals were stored.

They were in a two-shelf section. I started with the 1960 edition and worked my way through 1961 to 1962. There they were, both of them, 1962 graduates. One had three years of football to his credit, two years of basketball. The other had followed a different route, as junior prom chairman, the glee club, senior prom chairman.

I had guessed it would be one of my new friends. I hadn't been sure of which one until now.

Mrs. Vogel came over to ask, "Did you locate your Frank Martino?"

"I did. And the name of his local friend I needed. Thank you for your help, Mrs. Vogel."

"I was glad to do it," she said. "I do hope Bernie will have you over to the house for poker some night."

That would be the day—or night. I smiled, thanked her again and left.

19

WHAT I HAD was a name. What I didn't have was a case.

Ladies and gentlemen of the jury, the evidence that has been presented here clearly proves that X went to high school with Y. Can there now be any reasonable doubt left in your minds that Y is the murderer of Mrs. Marner?

No prosecutor would consider what I had learned even a sensible approach to a conviction. The court did not deal in theories or scenarios. The court dealt in facts.

The sun was out in all its fury now. My Detroit junker waited patiently on the school parking lot for further instructions.

Mary Serano might have some answers, but I didn't relish meeting her husband again so soon. The school was close to the underprivileged area of town; I headed down into it, searching for a red Porsche. Maybe Skip had come up with something.

No Porsche, no Skip, no luck.

It was a slow morning at Trinity Liquors. Moses and his son were playing darts.

"If you shoot baskets like you throw darts," Moses was telling his son, "you're gonna end up in the liquor business."

He turned his head to smile at me. "You come to open a charge account?"

"Not today. I want to use your phone book."

I looked up the name. The address was Ellis Lane.

"Where is Ellis Lane?" I asked.

Moses shrugged, still throwing darts.

His son said, "It's a little goat path that leads off Chapparal Road, about a quarter of a mile beyond Avalon Avenue."

That was up in the hills, but less than a mile from Kelly's Kourt.

Moses said, "I hear around you got Barney Leeds sweating. You didn't use my name, I hope?"

"No. I fed him a Tishkin lead. Do you think Barney might break?"

"It wouldn't take much bending to break him. If he had any guts, he wouldn't be paying off, would he?" He hit a bull's-eye and bowed to the nonexistent acclaim. "You know anything more about what happened to Mrs. Marner?"

"A little. But not enough to take into court. Moses, thank you again for last night. And you, too, Jerry."

"Anytime," Moses said. "Anytime you need muscle, here's the place to come for it. Booze, too. We deliver all over town."

"I'll bet you don't stock Einlicher."

"I stock it and I drink it. And for the man who put Locum in the hospital, I'll sell it to you at cost."

"I'll pay the regular markup. Deliver a couple of cases to my house. If nobody's home, leave them in the garage." I gave him my address and went out.

Padilla to San Valdesto Street, on that all the way to the home of Mary Serano, waitress, bookie, doting mother. The car was an oven; it was a relief to get out of it. Her Cadillac was in the driveway. The Camaro wasn't in sight.

"You look beat," Mary said. "Come in."

"I hope your happy-go-lucky hubby isn't home," I said.

"That slob is now in Phoenix," she said. "He's back in the welding business with his idiot brother. I gave him enough to buy a half interest and told him if he ever showed up in this town again, I'd turn my cousins loose on him."

"A wise decision," I said. "I've come for help."

"Come in, come in. I have news from down south about Patty. She went to see my brother down there and his wife phoned me."

"Great! Maybe if she learns you have dumped smiley, she'll be more eager to come home."

"That's what I want to talk with you about," she said. "A nice cold beer, maybe? I bought some better stuff than that swill Pete drank."

"Not Einlicher, by any chance?"

"No. Is that good? This is Bechtel's Bavarian. It was more than two dollars a bottle, but I thought you might drop in."

We were in the living room now. "You thought I might drop in and you could talk me into going down to Los Angeles?"

"I'll get the beer," she said.

When she brought it, I asked, "Why don't you go down and get her?"

"They don't know where she is. She didn't tell them much."

"That national firm that looked for her this spring," I said, "is much better equipped to find her than I am."

"They didn't find her, did they?"

"She probably wasn't down there then." I sipped the beer. It was delicious, very close to Einlicher.

"Don't just stand there," she said. "Sit down and drink your beer and we'll talk."

"Yes, ma'am," I said humbly. "I don't want to wind up as a welder in Phoenix." I sat down.

"I have enough to retire on now," she told me. "You tell Patty when you find her that I'll travel with her, this time. You tell her we'll go to Europe together, or any other place she wants to go."

"Yes, ma'am."

"I don't care what your fee is, understand? I'll pay it."

"No fee," I said, "if I decide to go."

"And when you come back," she said, "we'll go together to visit my friends in town who might help you find the person who killed Mrs. Marner. They all owe me. And they all know my cousins know they owe me."

"Did your cousins ever mention a man named Frank Martino?"

"Never. Well, Mr. Callahan?"

"Call me Brock," I said. "I'll go."

She gave me her brother's name and address. If I needed the addresses of her other relatives in that area, he would have them. All she had was their names. Her brother also had a lot of pictures of Patty.

Jan wasn't home when I got there. I left her a note, explaining that I had to make a hurried trip to Los Angeles on business. I would phone her. And then I thought of Otis Locum—and added that it might be wise for her to stay with the Lunds until I got back.

I threw some socks and shirts and shorts into a small grip, and took an extra pair of slacks and a jacket on a hanger. I stopped at the bank for money enough, and headed for the combination frontage road and ramp that led into Highway 101.

This was not the wanderers' way station that the Main Street intersection was, but there was a pair of them standing on the side of the road waiting for a ride. Their sign read L.A.

I stopped and waved for them to come.

The boy was slim and tall and clean. The girl was not as tall, but slimmer and cleaner. "How far are you going?" the boy asked.

"All the way to L.A. Hop in."

They threw their knapsacks in the back and the girl got in to sit next to them. The boy sat in the bucket seat next to mine.

"Nice," he said. "Sixty-five, sixty-six?"

"Early sixty-five."

"Two hundred and eighty-nine cubes?"

I moved into gear and out into the traffic of the freeway. "You called it right. With Dalton four-barrel carb and Spelke high-turbulence heads. And old Norman Spelke himself personally reground the cams."

"Nice," he said again.

They seemed to be nice, too. "Where are you from?" I asked.

"Mill Valley."

"Both of you?"

He nodded. "My name is Don. My friend's name is Dianne."

"My name is Callahan," I said, "Brock Callahan. Glad to meet you. That's beautiful country around Mill Valley. Is this your first trip to Los Angeles?"

"This is our first trip anywhere together," he said. "We're kind of square. Do you live in Los Angeles?"

"No. I moved up to San Valdesto this spring."

"It's a pretty town," he said, "but too quiet, like Mill Valley."

I laughed. "Quiet and square—those are dirty words, aren't they?"

He said nothing. Dianne said, "Don wants to be an actor. It's hard to be that in Mill Valley."

"It's hard to be that anywhere," I said, "if you want to be paid for it. You folks hungry? It's almost lunchtime, and there's a great rib place on the other side of Ventura. Do you like barbecued ribs?"

"We haven't had breakfast yet," Don said. "Is this place expensive?"

"Not when I'm picking up the tab. You will be my guests."

We rode for about five minutes in silence. Then Don said, "Brock Callahan . . . ? Weren't you a football player? Aren't you in the Hall of Fame at Canton?"

"My name is, and my jersey. I'm right here, riding along old Highway 101 with a couple of runaway kids."

"We left a note," Don said. "My dad hated you."

"He must be a 49er fan."

"Is he ever! Are you a coach now?"

"No. I'm a retired private investigator. I'm going to Los Angeles on an errand for a friend of mine. She wants me to talk her daughter into coming home."

A silence, and then Dianne said, "Your friend wouldn't be my mother, would she?"

"Not unless your mother is a waitress in San Valdesto."

She said, "Sorry. That was dumb of me. Does this girl want to be an actress?"

"I doubt it. She left home two years ago, when she was fifteen. Her last job was at a massage parlor in San Valdesto. Maybe she thought she could earn more working that Sunset Boulevard trade."

"And her mother wants *her* back?"

"Mothers are strange people," I said. "I've worked for a few of them when I was active. Let's talk about something else."

We didn't talk about anything all the way to Ronny's Rib Rendezvous. They were thinking and I was hoping. I was mostly hoping that they were thinking.

At Ronny's the waiter said, "Cocktail first, sir?"

"A double bourbon on the rocks," I said. "How about you two?"

Don looked at Dianne and both of them looked doubtfully at me. "Beer?" Don asked.

"Do you have your ID cards with you?" the waiter asked.

They stared at the tabletop.

I said, "Change my order to one double bourbon and two beers. Einlicher, if you serve it."

"Sir—"

"I am not only extremely muscular," I told him, "I am also a very impatient and thirsty man. We will order our lunch after I get my drinks."

The waiter went away, and Don smiled. Dianne said, "Mucho macho, just like your father, Don."

"Dad's not in the Hall of Fame," he said.

"Neither is Einstein," I said. "Have you had much experience as an actor?"

"In high school. We graduated in June."

"There must be a lot of little theater groups in an area like Mill Valley."

"I don't know. I suppose. Yes, there are."

"I read in the *Los Angeles Times* last week that only two percent of the members of the Screen Actors' Guild were currently working, and they're pros."

He smiled. "Yes, father."

"Okay," I said. "It's none of my damned business. But I remember some of the girls I finally found for their parents. Two of them were in the morgue.''

The waiter brought our drinks and we all ordered ribs. ''And three more beers,'' I added.

''Yes, sir,'' he said, and went quietly away.

''One girl I found had to be identified by her dental work,'' I went on. ''Even in that dry desert air, she was so badly decomposed that—''

''Please!'' Dianne said. ''Enough! We get your point.''

We ate in silence, we drank our beer. We climbed into the car again and went back to the freeway. Silence. Past Oxnard, starting the big climb at Camarillo Springs.

Up, up, up. . . . Past the crawling trucks, the tiny-engine foreign cars, groaning in third gear, the campers, the trailers.

At the crest, the San Fernando Valley was spread out below us. An ugly yellow blanket was blotting out the sun.

''My God, what's that?'' Dianne asked. ''There must be a fire somewhere!''

''That,'' I told her, ''is Los Angeles smog. Welcome to the home of the stars.''

''Don,'' she said. ''Oh, Don—''

''So we'll find a job and get enough to get home on,'' he said. ''We're down to nine dollars, Dianne.''

At the bus station in the San Fernando Valley, I bought them two tickets for San Francisco, and gave Don a double sawbuck. ''Take a cab from San Francisco,'' I said. ''Go home in style.''

''If you'll give me your address,'' he said, ''I'll—''

''Forget it. Go home and learn your trade, whatever that is. You sounded like an engineer to me.''

"I'm a pretty good mechanic," he said. "I've rebuilt a couple of old Jags, and sold them."

"Could I kiss you?" Dianne asked.

"If you don't think it would excite you too much."

She kissed me, he shook my hand, and then they had to hurry for the bus, already loading.

I stood there. People sat on the benches and read, or ate their lunches out of paper bags. Some bought tickets, some boarded buses, some got off. Not one of them had the grace to walk up and pin a Good Samaritan medal on me.

20

VINCENT BATTAGLIA was Mary Serano's oldest brother, a man of about sixty. He was short and stocky, as were his wife and two sons. Their daughter, Mary, was neither short nor stocky. Vincent had married late; the kids were still living at home.

In descending order, by ages, they were: Vincent Junior, 17, Mary, 16, and Tony, 15. Vincent hadn't wasted any time, once he deserted his bachelorhood.

They lived in a three-bedroom, bath-and-a-half, cream-colored stucco house on National Boulevard, near the Santa Monica Airport.

I met Mrs. Battaglia first. She answered the door to my ring. "Mr. Callahan!" she said. "When Mary told me yesterday that you were coming here, I thought my husband would have a heart attack. You're staying for dinner, of course?"

"If you insist. Mary told you yesterday?"

She nodded.

"But I didn't even tell her I was coming here until about four hours ago."

"She said you would come. She said she knew you would."

"She must have the gift of prophecy."

Mrs. Battaglia played it straight. "She has. Her mother told me she was born with the veil. Come in."

Here, as in the one-room home of Jesus Gonzales, there was a crucifix on the living-room wall. The furniture was dark, upholstered in brown mohair. Lace doilies protected the areas most likely to soil. The few pictures were religious scenes, including the Last Supper. I felt a wave of nostalgia wash over me; I had grown up in this kind of house in Long Beach.

"I have coffee on," she said. "But maybe you'd rather have something cold?"

"Coffee will be fine," I said.

She brought a five-by-seven portrait of Patty with my coffee. "Isn't she beautiful?"

She had Mary's big eyes and olive skin and shining black hair. "She certainly is," I said. "What did she tell you when she was here?"

"Nothing much. But she told my daughter she was going to be in a movie, starting this week. I don't know why she didn't tell me more about it."

I could guess why. I asked, "Does your daughter know the name of the firm making the movie?"

"I don't think so. My oldest boy, Vince, probably does. He was teasing Patty about it."

"Do you know where Patty is staying?"

She shook her head. "Today's kids—"

I sipped my coffee.

"Patty used to come here for a couple of weeks every summer. What a sweet girl she was! But after she turned fifteen—" Her face hardened. "Of course, with that father of hers—"

"Mary has sent him packing," I said. "Didn't you know that?"

"No. When did it happen?"

"It must have happened since she talked with you yesterday. She told me this morning. If Patty gets in touch with you again, be sure to tell her that."

"That could make a difference," she said. "Nobody in the family could ever understand what she saw in that man."

Mary came home first, acknowledged the introduction politely and went to her room.

The boys came together, were just as polite and went out in back to throw basketballs into the hoop over the garage door.

The master of the house gave me more attention. He stood in the middle of the living room, his hands on his hips, and stared at me, a real ham. "I never thought I would live to see this day," he said. "You honor this house, sir."

That was his opening. For the next hour and a half he talked and I listened. He must have seen every Rams home game since the club moved to California. I had the feeling that he remembered every play of every game.

Dinner was all high-caloric Italian food: canneloni, cacciatore, even macaroni in the minestrone. Young Mary was the only person at the table who ate sparingly.

When we had finished, I said to Vince Junior, "Could I talk with you alone for a few minutes?"

His face was guarded. He looked at his father.

"Do it," his father said.

We went to the room he shared with Tony. I asked, "What's the name of that movie company Patty is going to work for?"

"Why should I tell you? So you can drag her back to that house? Patty is a friend of mine."

"If you're really a friend of hers, you'll tell me. Your aunt dumped that slob she married. She sent him to Phoenix, to go into business with his brother. If he ever comes back to San Valdesto, her cousins will cut him up for dog food."

He looked at me suspiciously.

"That's God's honest truth, Vince. Your aunt is retiring and she wants to travel and she wants Patty to go with her."

He remained stubbornly silent.

"If Patty doesn't want to go home," I said, "I won't crowd her. I promise you that. Don't you realize where she's heading, man?"

He stared at me for a few more seconds before he said, "Adult Art Cinema. They've got an office in Hollywood, I guess, but they make their pictures out in some house near Malibu."

"You thought that was something to tease Patty about?"

"I was trying to shame her in front of the folks. When we were alone, I tried to talk her out of it."

"Thank you," I said. "And trust me," I added.

"I have to, now," he said.

His father wanted me to spend the night there, but I explained that I had people to see. I promised them I would tell Mary to phone them if my mission was successful.

Back in the car, I headed for Heinie's. I missed that bum—and besides, he was a porno movie fan.

There were five men at the bar, four of them horseplayers going over their handicap sheets together.

"The Rock!" he said. "What you doing in town?"

"Looking up old friends. As a connoisseur of dirty pictures, have you ever heard of a firm called Adult Art Cinema?"

"Yuck!" he said. "Who wants to look at freaks? All their pictures are loaded with those Muscle Beach weirdos. I go to look at women. You ain't signing up with *them*, are you?"

"Heinie!"

"Sorry. I forgot you don't need that kind of money now. Einlicher?"

"Please. You mean there are no women in their pictures?"

"Young girls, mostly. Just kids. They get 'em cheap, I suppose. And the things those kids go through with those muscle-bound nitwits—my stomach isn't *that* strong, buddy."

Later, from the same wall phone I had used to inform Jan of my inheritance, I called our house. No answer.

I phoned the Lunds' house. Jan was there. "What happened?" she asked.

"It was an emergency—kind of."

"Chief Harris phoned you and Lieutenant Vogel phoned twice."

"Call Vogel at home," I told her. "Tell him I'm down here trying to find Patty Serano for her mother. And for us. Why were he and the chief looking for me?"

"I couldn't understand it. Something about Otis Locum being out of the hospital. Is that why you wanted me to stay here?"

"That was the main reason."

"And who is Patty Serano?"

"She is the daughter of a woman who could be helpful to us in our investigation."

"Where are you now?"

"In a restaurant. I'll be at the Shamrock West in half an hour, if they have a room for me. If they haven't, I'll phone you back."

They had a room, and I had a good night's sleep. I had tried to find Adult Art Cinema in the phone book before I went to bed. There was no listing. They could be too new to be listed or too cheap to install a phone. More likely, they had a private number.

In the morning, I called one of my Hollywood haunts, Mimi's Grotto. It was run by a great lady who specialized in bad food and good banter. Mimi answered the phone.

I said, "This is Brock. Has Amos come in for breakfast yet?"

"Not yet. Where have *you* been lately, you bum?"

"I'm retired. I'm only in town for the day—I hope. Do you have Amos's phone number?"

"I'm one of the few who have." She gave it to me.

Amos had an unlisted number and specialized in selling unlisted numbers, plus a variety of other services.

I told him what I wanted.

"Adult Art Cinema?" he said. "I can get it for you. It will cost you a tenner."

"Okay. I'll mail you a check. Or I could leave your money here at the desk?"

"The desk? Where? At the Mission? I've had your rubber checks before, Brock."

"You cheap fink," I said. "Okay. Come to the hotel and I'll buy you breakfast and give you the ten. I'll probably need you for more work today."

"What hotel?"

"The Shamrock, room 138. Hurry! I'm getting hungry."

Unlisted numbers was only one of Amos Gilchrist's services. Angles was another. He was a slick and innovative man. He had learned early in his career that the police took a more kindly view of his profession if he cheated crooks instead of marks.

The crooks didn't, of course. Which meant that he was also a brave man.

He was there before I had finished shaving. He looked around my Shamrock suite and said, "You must be on a big one, if the sucker's paying for this."

"I'm paying for this," I told him sternly. "Do you want to eat in here or in the dining room?"

"In here? What are we, hermits? When I eat at the Shamrock, I want people to see me. Where'd you get those threads?"

I was putting on my new sports jacket. "From my tailor, where else?"

"Since when do they have tailors down at the Salvation Army? What goes on here?"

I told him my story, from Homer Gallup's demise to Mary Serano's request. And added, "If you want to check my solvency, you can phone Grant Robbins, of Weede, Robbins, McCulloch and Adler. I'm sure you have heard of them."

"Of course. But why would I check you? Haven't we always trusted each other?"

I stared at him.

"So, all right! This morning I happened to need the ten in cash. Mimi has put me on a cash basis, and I was hungry, Brock!"

"I'll feed you in a few minutes. What do you know about this Adult Art outfit? Do you think they might know who we are?"

He shook his head. "Not unless they're football fans with long memories. They only came to town a month ago. They're out of Newark."

"I see. Then their number isn't unlisted. You called information!"

"But you didn't. Your money hasn't made you much smarter, has it?"

"Let's eat," I said, "and talk."

Twenty-nine dollars later, we were back in the room and Amos was on the phone with a Mr. Barry Holly of Adult Art Cinema.

The way Amos explained it, there was this quirky rich guy from San Valdesto who thought there must be a great profit potential in the kind of pictures Adult Art Cinema produced. Would it

be possible for him to talk with Mr. Holly today?
Perhaps we could all meet for lunch at the Shamrock?

A pause, and then, "All right. You're on Ivar
Street, aren't you?"

Another pause, and Amos said, "His name is B.
Langtry Callahan. His friends call him Loony Lan-
ny. He lives outside of town, in Montevista."
Another pause. "Thank you." He hung up.

"He's too busy to have lunch with us. We have
an eleven-o'clock appointment. You're not still
driving that little yellow junker, are you?"

I nodded.

"Call the desk," he said. "Have the man rent us
a Rolls with a chauffeur for the day. And call room
service for some coffee. We have some thinking to
do, and you're not very good at it."

"Yes, sir," I said.

At ten-forty-five we were rolling down Sunset
Boulevard in a silver Rolls-Royce with a black top,
driven by a liveried chauffeur. "You could probably afford one of these now," Amos said. "But
you've always had a lot of peasant in you, haven't
you?"

"If you mean I've always paid my way, if you
mean I never got low enough to stiff some poor
woman out of a meal—"

"Cut it out! Mimi is about as poor as an Arab oil
sheikh. I just happen to be going through a bad
period."

"You could try honest labor."

"Look who's talking! Morality lectures from a
peeper, yet."

Silence from me. And from him.

After a couple blocks of it, he said, "Name me
somebody I hurt who didn't have it coming. Name
me one, you bastard."

"When you name me one peasant who ever bought you a fifteen-dollar breakfast. I didn't know you were so sensitive."

He laughed. "And I didn't know you were. Hell, man, there are popes who have had lower moral standards than ours."

"Not any recent popes."

"I'm sorry. I forgot you were Catholic. Buddies, Brock?"

"Blood brothers," I said. "You bastard."

The offices of Adult Art Cinema were not impressive, on the first floor of an old stucco building on Ivar. I thought the chauffeur's nose twitched when Amos told him to keep the car in view of the former store-window front of the place.

"We're lucky," Amos said. "This kind of operation usually has that window boarded over. They probably don't shoot their pictures here."

There were no chairs in the waiting room, only benches. The muscle boys in their tight pants were sitting in there, some old hookers in tighter pants—and the kids. The sweet, dumb kids hoping for stardom on any stairway available to them.

The office of Barry Holly, vice-president in charge of casting, was on the right, off the front of the room. A prim-looking woman of about fifty in a simple gray dress sat at a small desk next to the door.

"Amos Gilchrist and Mr. Callahan," Amos said. "We have an appointment."

"Go right in, gentlemen," she said.

His office wasn't much of a change from the waiting room, except that there were chairs in there. Barry Holly stood up from behind his desk as we entered.

He was wide at the hips and narrow across the shoulders, with a thin ferretlike face, sparse hair, and eyes of faded blue. "Which one of you is Mr. Callahan?" he asked.

I reach across the desk to shake his hand.

"From San Valdesto, I understand," he said. "A beautiful town."

"A little on the quiet side for me. Do all those young chicks out there work for you?"

"Not yet," he said. "Be seated, gentlemen."

It was probably the first time in our lives that Amos or I had been called gentlemen twice in two minutes. We sat down.

So did Barry. "I understand from Mr. Gilchrist that you'd like to invest in a picture."

I smirked at him. "Why not. Gives me a chance to meet the stars."

He smiled. "Did you have a figure in mind, Mr. Callahan?"

I shrugged. "Not too heavy. Fifty, sixty thousand, until I see how it pays off. I suppose that's peanuts."

"Possibly to M.G.M.," he said. "Not to us. Most of our pictures are low-budget productions. But they do have the potential for a substantial return of investment. I hope you understand we can't guarantee anything?"

I nodded. "Mr. Gilchrist has explained that to me." I glanced at Amos and looked back at Holly. "I, uh, wasn't completely frank with him. There was a girl up there in San Valdesto, a girl named Patty Serano that I've.... What I mean, I kind of thought if *she* was in the picture—"

"Patty Serano," he told me, "signed a contract with us almost a week ago. Where did you learn she was working with us?"

"From her Aunt Rose. Is she here now?"

"Unfortunately, no. She's on location up in Malibu. They're starting to shoot tonight. I have an idea—why don't you and Mr. Gilchrist drive up there tonight, and we can have a sort of round-table discussion. Our president, Michael Ducasse, will be there and maybe we can come to some arrangement profitable to us all."

"That sounds good to me," I said. "How about you, Amos?"

"Fine. What time, Mr. Holly?"

"About nine?"

"We'll be there," I said.

He gave us the address and we went out into the smoggy but cleaner air of Ivar Street.

21

OVER LUNCH at the hotel, Amos said, "I'll nose around town this afternoon and get what line I can on those creeps."

I smiled. "And if you find out they're mob connected, you won't be back. Maybe I'd better pay you now."

"Mob connected? An outfit that chintzy? But I could use a little walking-around money."

I gave him three twenties and told him, "If that girl goes back to San Valdesto with me tonight, there's five hundred more in it for you."

He shook his head. "Man, have you changed! The way you used to chisel me—"

"I was dealing with a chiseler. I had to play his game."

"I suppose," he said, "the thought never occurred to you to play it straight. A contract with a seventeen-year-old girl isn't valid unless her parents sign it."

"Breaking her contract wouldn't bring her home. I want her *home.*"

He studied me suspiciously. "You lust for this kid?"

"I've never even seen her. You have a dirty mind, Amos."

He nodded. "I grew up in a dirty neighborhood. I think I'll have another piece of that cheesecake."

When he left, he said, "Why don't you drive out

to that address in Malibu and check out the roads? We may have to leave in a hurry."

A drive along the ocean wouldn't be a bad way to kill the afternoon. I took his advice. When I came out onto the Coast Road, the ocean breeze was cool, the smog at a minimum.

Past the Palisades, past Topanga, enjoying the air. Gehringer Road led off the highway to the right, a few hundred feet short of where the road to the Colony led off to the left. It was a steep, winding and narrow road.

The mailbox at the address Holly had given us was on the road. The name on the box was Ducasse, and the paint was faded. Ducasse couldn't have come out here a month ago from Newark; even the California sun couldn't bleach the letters that fast.

His house was high above the road, his entire acreage bordered with a chain-link fence that looked new to me. The double gate was locked. We could leave in a hurry—if we had a helicopter.

Driving down again, I wondered if my old friend Marvin Burns still worked at the Malibu Sheriff's Station.

He did. He was knee-deep in paperwork, as usual. I don't believe Deputy Marvin Burns had ever used his revolver, except on the target range.

"I thought you had moved to San Valdesto," he said. "Somebody told me that."

"I did move. I'm only in town for the day. I thought I'd drop in and buy you a beer."

He studied me. "And what do you think a beer will buy you?"

"How about two beers?"

"Aagh!" he said. "You...! Okay, I guess I can knock off for half an hour."

At the Tender Tavern (owned by Terence Tender), Marv said, "I understand a couple of the big

boys have moved to your little sanctuary to retire.
Dons, weren't they?"

"I guess. Harris is still in charge, though, I'm
sure."

"He's a lot of cop," Marv said. "Ornery old bastard, isn't he?"

I nodded. I asked, "What do you know about a
man named Michael Ducasse?"

He shrugged. "Nothing much. He's obviously
rich and I hear he's weird. Why?"

"Do you mean sexually weird?"

"Why do you want to know? You mean because
he rents out his house to those porno movie
creeps?"

"You know *that*, and nothing's being done about
it?"

"Cut it out, Callahan! We go to court and their
shyster proves their films have redeeming social
value. Which means we have wasted some more of
the taxpayers' money."

"How long has Ducasse lived in that house?"

"As long as I've been out here. At least twelve
years. Why?"

"He is the president of Adult Art Cinema. And
the word I get is that his associates moved out here
only a month ago from Newark."

"Why the hell should you care? I thought you
were retired."

"I'm still a citizen."

"Oh, Jesus! I'll have another beer."

After tender Terence Tender brought it and went
away, I said, "They have just signed a seventeen-
year-old girl to a contract without her parents' con-
sent. Isn't that illegal?"

"Probably. But that would make it a civil case,
not criminal. Sue him, if you're an interested
party."

"I take it you're not an interested party."

"Not me. I'm just a crooked cop, drinking while on duty. If you think I'm cynical, I am. The world's gone crazy in the last couple of years."

When I left him at the station, he said, "Thanks for that Newark tip. Maybe *they* have records. Ducasse hasn't."

I was back at the hotel at four o'clock, and spent an hour in the pool. A little after five, Amos phoned. "Are we eating there?"

"Unless you want to put me on your tab at Mimi's?"

"Be nice! That heap of yours hasn't a very big rear seat, has it?"

"No."

"We'll take my car," he said. "There's a possibility Holly checked our credentials after we left him and found out you were a private eye. So I hired a couple of guys for backup."

"Are they going to eat here, too?"

"Neither one owns a tie. They'll meet us there at eight-thirty." He paused. "Outside."

OUTSIDE WAS THE PROPER PLACE for them. They both would have marred the elegant decor of the Shamrock lobby. They were high and wide and ugly, with matching cauliflower ears, scar tissue above the eyes and flattened noses. They both wore sweat-stained T-shirts and faded jeans.

One was black and one white; Amos was an Equal Opportunity Employer. The white one was named Joe, the black one Jack. That, Amos informed me, was all I needed to know.

We climbed into his highly polished twelve-year-old Cadillac and purred off toward Malibu.

I told him what Marv Burns had told me about Ducasse.

Amos had more: "The story I got, he has a yen for twelve-year-old girls. The Newark boys need the free rent. So they give him the title of president, find him a few twelve-year-old girls, and they're in business."

It was getting dark now; headlights came at us in a constant stream along the Coast Road. I said, "I've got to talk with Patty alone some way. I have to tell her her father's no longer in the house."

"We'll think of something," he said. "Maybe we won't have to. I talked with a couple of case-hardened hookers today who walked out on them. Those muscle freaks dream up some sick stuff."

We climbed the winding road. The gate was open. There was an old station wagon parked in front of the big house and a black Continental with New Jersey license plates.

Amos told Jack and Joe, "Stay out of sight. If we need you, I'll signal."

"How?" Jack asked.

"I'll think of a way. Just be ready." We walked to the front door and Amos rang the bell.

Barry Holly opened the door. "Good evening, gentlemen."

I hope so, I thought.

"Come in," he said.

The living room led off to the right from the small entrance foyer. We would be in the front part of the house, a comforting thought. There were two men waiting for us in the living room.

One of them had his back to us. He was staring out a front window. The other sat in an enormous, black satin upholstered armchair. He got up as we entered.

The man at the window turned toward him. "That's some view you've got, Michael."

He was a big man, with one of those blue black beards no razor can ever cut close enough to hide.

Michael Ducasse was shorter, thinner, darker and less frightening. He could have been a hairdresser. "Thank you, Al." He turned to us. "Welcome to my home," he said. "You can call me Mike. This is my friend, Albert Spicuzzi."

We shook hands all around.

"Call me Al," Spicuzzi said.

"My friends call me Lanny," I told him.

"Okay, Lanny," Spicuzzi said. "So let's sit and let's talk."

Amos sat on a hassock near a front window. I sat on a couch next to Holly, Ducasse sank back again into the satin chair. Big Al didn't follow his own suggestion; he stood next to Ducasse's chair.

He said, "Barry tells me you'd like to back a picture with Patty Serano starring in it."

"Well, not back it completely," I said. "I'm sure you can't make a picture for fifty or sixty thousand dollars."

"We can try," Al said. "Patty a friend of yours?"

I shook my head. "I only met her once. It was in a massage parlor in San Valdesto. She probably doesn't even remember me."

"You met her *once*? You mean you didn't go back?"

"I went back last week. But she wasn't there."

"And you followed her down here?"

"Not really. I was in town on business and I looked up her Aunt Rose, and...." I shrugged.

He studied me. I felt like a bug on a pin. He looked at Holly. "Is Patty still here?"

Holly nodded. "But they're shooting. We could wait."

Al shook his head. "Get her."

Holly got up and went through the foyer toward the back of the house. In a few minutes we could hear them coming our way. Not their footsteps; what we heard was a girl's complaining voice.

Holly was holding Patty's elbow when they came into the living room. She was wearing a terry-cloth robe, and probably nothing else.

She ignored all of us but Ducasse. "Mr. Ducasse," she said angrily, "I want out!"

He smiled at her. "You'd prefer to go back to jail? We bailed you out of there, Patty, and we can send you back."

"All right, then, get me a new male lead. Somebody human. That filthy Angelo is right out of sickville. I won't work with him!"

"Who's Angelo?" Spicuzzi asked.

"Angelo Arrapopulus," Holly said. "Remember him, the wrestler? He used to be pretty big out here."

"Never heard of him," Spicuzzi said. "Get him."

I looked at Amos, and Amos looked nervously at me. We both knew Angelo Arrapopulus and he had reason to remember me. I had worked for his wife. I had obtained ample grounds for her divorce from Angelo, enough to get her about seventy percent of his assets at the time.

"Do we need him?" I asked. "I'm sure we can find somebody else Patty would be happier working with."

"We need him now," Al said. "I want to get this fuss straightened out right now."

Amos's eyes had left mine and were scanning the room. He might have been looking for a convenient exit. He could have been looking for a weapon. Knowing Amos, I had to guess it was an exit. He is a brave man in some ways, but he loathes physical violence.

Holly didn't have to go and get Angelo; he was now standing in the doorway from the foyer, also wearing a robe. He glared at Ducasse. "Are we working with virgins?" he asked. And then he saw me. "What is he doing here?"

"Mr. Callahan," Holly informed, "is a potential investor in our company. He's from San Valdesto."

"Like hell," Angelo said. "He's a lousy peeper from L.A. He's the bastard that got the goods on me for my ex. Brock Callahan? You guys don't remember him?"

Amos and I were suddenly the center of attention. Al looked between us, back and forth. Then, "You two can leave quietly now or leave on stretchers later. You decide."

"And I'm going with them," Patty said.

"The hell you are," Al said.

"The hell she isn't," I said, and stood up.

"I'll get Franky," Angelo said. "We'll take care of this jerk for you, Mr. Ducasse."

That was when Amos found what he had been looking for. It wasn't an exit or a weapon. It was a signal. He picked up a heavy marble lamp from a nearby end table and threw it through the front window.

22

GLASS FELL QUIETLY on the soft carpeting and tinkled off the end table. Big Al came for me. Amos would have been a softer match, but Amos was no longer in sight.

"Franky!" Angelo shouted, and came over to help Al.

Two against one.... They were muckers, like Otis. What has happened to American tradition? I would have gone up clean against Al, man to man. John Wayne was dead; somebody had to carry on the tradition.

The lamp I hit Al with was smaller than the one Amos had thrown through the window, but it was cut glass and it cut up his forehead pretty good. The blood running down over his eyes could have been the reason his looping overhand right missed me by a foot.

I put my own right into his nose to hamper his breathing, as Angelo circled to get a side shot at me.

Together, they could have taken me—maybe. But from the doorway Jack called, "Hey, Angelo, baby! This way. You're mine, Angie!"

He came in, as Angelo moved toward him. Another hulk, probably Franky, came running into the foyer—and into Joe.

The grapple and groan boys against club fighters? Forget it. This wasn't Friday night at the

Olympic on Channel Five. This was the real world.

Al had no partner now. It was man to man and I honored the tradition. I didn't try to disfigure him, only to make sure he would spend the rest of his life in pain. As I have mentioned before, I like kids.

Joe and Jack hadn't been active in the ring for some time. They were overdoing it a little. There was no reason for them to stand there and kick unconscious men.

I pulled them away, and asked, "Where's Amos?"

"In the car with the girl," Jack said. "Let's get out of here before the fuzz come."

Holly and Ducasse were not in sight. Like Amos, they probably were not physical. Or maybe they were calling the police, though I doubted it.

Amos had the engine running. Patty was in the seat beside him. I slid in next to her, as Jack and Joe climbed into the back seat.

"Move it, gutless," I said.

He swung the big car in an arc and headed down the driveway. "Gutless? What the hell you talking about?"

"I missed you during the action."

"You dumb mick! Somebody had to get Patty's clothes for her, didn't he? You want to take the girl home naked?"

"I'm not going home," Patty said. "That is the last place I'm going."

"The decision is yours," I said. "But would you talk with me about it before you decide?"

"Talk won't change my mind."

We were about three blocks from the house when we heard the sound of a siren below, and saw the flashing red light as it came around a curve.

"Stay well over to the right," I told Amos. "This is a narrow road."

"The law," he informed me, "reads that all drivers are required to stop. What kind of driver do you think I am?"

He pulled over onto the grass in a flat area and turned off the car lights, as the county black and white came around the turn below us.

When it went past us, he turned on the lights and started down again. "I can't believe those creeps would call the law."

"It was probably neighbors. But they might have. The sheriff's department knows what's going on there, and they haven't busted them. That makes them legitimate."

"Don't worry about them," Patty said. "I know enough about them to keep them from starting anything. There are two twelve-year-old girls up there right now."

"Did they let you play with their dolls?" Amos asked.

"Shut up!" she said.

From the back, Jack said, "I'm glad I got my licks in on Angelo. My wife thinks he was the prettiest thing on the tube since Gorgeous George. Them wrestlers are sure sickening, aren't they?"

"Grotesque," Patty said.

There was no more dialogue all the way to the hotel. There, in the parking garage, I gave Amos his five hundred and Jack and Joe the fifty each he had promised them.

They left, and I asked Patty, "Are you hungry? Would you like to go someplace and eat—and talk?"

She said, "I haven't eaten since two o'clock. I know a great place for burgers and shakes right near here. But talking isn't going to change anything."

At Arnold's she sipped her shake and munched her hamburger. I sipped my large Coke.

"Your mother wants to travel," I said. "She's retiring. She'll take you anyplace in the world you want to go."

"With *him*? No, thanks!"

"By him, do you mean your father?"

"He's not my father. I never told mom I knew that, but I do."

"Who told you?"

"He did. Mom was three months pregnant when he married her. He told me he married her as a favor, to give me a name."

"When did he tell you that?"

"Three years ago, when I was fourteen." She looked down at the table and up again at me. "The first time he took a pass at me."

"And you believed him?"

"Wouldn't you? Would you like to think your own father . . . ." She shivered and sniffed.

"He is now in Phoenix," I said. "He is in business with his brother down there. If he comes back to San Valdesto, your mother's cousins will give him reason to regret it."

She stared at me. "Is that the truth?"

"I swear to God it's the truth. And I'll promise you something else. If he comes back to town and your mother's cousins are busy, you call on me and I will personally castrate him."

She giggled. "You wouldn't do that!"

"Probably not. Are you ready to go home?"

"I'm ready," she said. "Wait until I finish my burger. I'll take the milk shake along to drink on the road."

A few miles short of Oxnard, I said, "Lenny Tishkin's back in town."

"Who cares? That's over!"

"He was asking for you at the Arden Massage Parlor."

"Oh, God! Does my mother know I worked there?"

"Not through me. I doubt if she knows it."

"That's where I would have wound up, if I'd stuck with Lenny."

"Instead," I said, "you wound up as an internationally famous star with the Adult Art Cinema studios."

"Shut up!"

I shut up.

This side of Ventura, she said, "I'm sorry. After all you went through to get me out of there, and the expense it will be to my mother—"

I said, "Don't you worry about Mary Serano. She's loaded. She's ready for Europe, first class all the way."

It was after midnight when we pulled up in front of her house, but there was a light showing through the living-room window.

From behind the locked front door, Mary asked, "Who is it?"

"It's me, mom," Patty answered. "Me and Mr. Callahan."

Hugs and tears, while I stood there. Then Mary broke free to say, "Come in. You can come in for a few minutes, can't you?"

"I'd better get home. I'll see you tomorrow."

"And you send me a bill," she said. "Never mind what you said. You send me a bill! You understand that?"

"I understand that. Sleep tight, both of you."

I had turned off onto Main Street, heading for

the highway intersection, when the police cruiser pulled up behind me, its red light flashing. I stopped and took out my driver's license.

One officer came to my side window, the other stayed near the cruiser. The one next to me said, "Mr. Brock Callahan?"

"Yes."

"Keep your hands in sight and step out of the car."

"Is this a joke?"

"Keep your hands in sight," he repeated, "and step out of the car."

I got out and went through the ritual, my hands on the top of my car, while he went through his feelies. Then he said, "I'll ride in your car to the station. My partner will follow."

"How do you know I haven't got a gun under my seat?"

"Mr. Callahan," he said in a patient voice, "all we do is follow orders. We got a call. We picked you up."

"And felt me up," I added. "Was that routine necessary?"

"Let's go," he said. "Do you know where the station is?"

"I've been working out of it for a week. I ought to. Am I supposed to be dangerous?"

"The dispatcher didn't say. Please, let's go!"

He was young and doing his duty. I didn't argue. We rode to the station and parked on the lot. He took me right to Captain Dahl's office.

"Well!" Dahl said. "The Montevista Avenger. Where have you been, Mr. Callahan?"

"I've been out of town. Is this one of your nasty ways to get back at Lund through me?"

"You don't know what happened?"

I didn't answer him.

"You may sit down," he said, "if you wish."

I sat down on the straight chair next to his desk.

"For two days," he said, "Otis Locum has been spreading the word around town that he's out to get you. So, three hours ago, when we found him dead, it's logical to guess that you might have got to him first. Is that logical to you?"

"Dead? How? Knife, gun . . . ? How?"

"He was found dead at the foot of that cliff across the road from his house. We have a witness who told us that she saw somebody push him off the cliff. Then that somebody drove away in a yellow car. You have a yellow car, do you not?"

"So does that hoodlum who threatened Mary Serano. Don't you think he might be a more logical suspect?"

"The woman said this was a *small* yellow car."

"Did she also notice the size of the man who pushed Locum?"

"No. She couldn't even be sure he was a man. It was foggy out there."

"That's some case you've got," I said.

"I didn't say I have a case. Right now, all I have are questions."

"I don't think I'd better give you any more answers," I said. "I think I need a lawyer."

"I'll phone one for you. Who do you want? Nowicki? Farini?"

I shook my head—and watched for his reaction when I said, "I want Paul Pontius."

All I could read on his face was surprise. "Pontius? He doesn't practice law anymore. He's retired."

"He's still licensed in California. Call him."

"Call a retired attorney at one o'clock at night?" He handed me the phone book. "The pleasure's all yours."

When Paul answered the phone and I told him what had happened, he said simply, "I see. I'll call you back."

He didn't. At least he didn't while I was at the station. But Dahl's phone rang in about five minutes.

Dahl said, "Yes, Chief.".Pause. "Yes, he told me he was out of town, but he didn't tell me that." Pause. "Yes, sir."

He hung up. "Okay, you can go, Callahan."

"I have to wait for Pontius to call back," I said.

"Go," he said. "Haven't you had enough trouble for tonight? Why didn't you tell me you were down in Malibu three hours ago?"

"Would it have made a difference? And how does the chief know that? Did Pontius tell him, or am I being followed?"

"For the third and last time, Callahan—go!"

It was too late to phone Jan now. I went home. I filled the tub with hot water and a tumbler with liquid corn and I soaked. About halfway through the corn, I realized the night had balanced out. I should have been picked up in Malibu and hadn't. I should not have been picked up here, and had.

23

I DIDN'T WAKE UP until nine o'clock. I phoned Jan, and she was home twenty minutes later. I was still in my robe, consuming four scrambled eggs and toasted sourdough bread when she came into the breakfast room.

"Welcome home," she said, and kissed me. "Now Mr. Locum won't dare show his face around here, will he?"

"Maybe his ghost. He's dead."

"How? When? How do you know?"

I told her how and when and how I knew and went on to relate a bowdlerized version of my adventures in Los Angeles, while she drank some of the coffee I had made.

When I had finished my stirring tale of gallantry and heroism, she said only, "You sure make lousy coffee. You should have waited until I got home."

"Oh, God!" I said.

"I'm not that trivial, dummy. I said that because I decided not to say what I wanted to say. And I'm not going to say it. You're safe at home."

"Nobody's safe. At home or anywhere else."

"Let's not fight. Skip had a message for you. I wrote it down to make sure I got it right."

The message was this: A friend of Skip's, with his female friend, were parked along Chapparal Road the same night Jesus Gonzales was supposed to have left town at eight o'clock. It was ten o'clock when this couple had seen Jesus walking up Chapparal Road. Both Skip's friend and his friend's friend would confirm this. Skip had added that he didn't know why or if this information was important, but the couple were friends of Jesus, and they had thought it was.

"Will it help you?" Jan asked.

I nodded.

"Are you going downtown again today?"

"Yes."

Danning Villwock, the hermit, the retired parole officer, the marijuana advocate, lived off Chapparal Road. But that was a long walk up to his place. Jesus might have turned off at Ellis Lane, that road Moses Jones's son had called a goat path.

I had my name. I still didn't have any hard evidence. Mary had her daughter back; she didn't need me anymore. But I was sure that Mary, as I did, believed in owing and being owed.

Jan was out in front, chipping again with one of my old clubs, when I left. She was a natural, dropping six out of ten shots into a redwood tub only thirty inches across from twelve yards away.

"You're beautiful," I said. "You're ready for the L.P.G.A. tour. You're remarkable."

"That's what Skip said. He said I'm already better than both of you."

"That would still put you two light years away from the L.P.G.A. tour," I told her. "I won't be home for lunch."

"Neither will I. I'm having a one-o'clock lesson at the club."

Fight bravely on, Jan. The enemy is at the gate. I kissed her and went down to the real world again.

Helms's office was full of smoke, as usual. "You ought to hang a ham in here," I said. "It should cure pretty good."

He shook his head sadly. "Lippy is home! The chief has been asking for you. You'd better get in there."

The chief was at his desk, reading some papers and frowning. "You're back," he said. "I suppose you were surprised when I told Dahl to release you last night."

"Not really. Not after I phoned Pontius and he phoned you."

He half rose from his chair. "What are you suggesting?"

"That's the way it was, wasn't it? I only repeated what happened."

"You are one arrogant son of a bitch," he said. "I've been called a lot of things, but nobody ever called me a crooked cop before."

"Neither did I. Who told you about the trouble I'd had in Malibu?"

"Your good friend Sergeant Marvin Burns from the Malibu Sheriff's Station. He phoned me around eleven o'clock."

"He was working two watches? He was on the day watch yesterday when I talked with him."

"He wasn't working. He called me from home. The boys who answered the call at that porno place got your name from somebody there, and they knew you were a friend of his. They phoned Sergeant Burns at home. He gave me a message to relay to you."

"Drop dead? Get lost?"

"You're not nearly as funny as you think you are, Callahan. He told me to tell you that he didn't like the way you worked, but to thank you, anyway. There were two twelve-year-old girls in that house."

"I know. Why did Captain Dahl have me picked up?"

"He made that clear to you, didn't he? Pretend you were Dahl, in charge of the night watch, knowing what he knew. Would you have sent out the call?"

"Yes, I guess. Okay, yes."

"And as for Paul Pontius phoning me," he went on in his grating voice, "he knows two people in this department, me and Lieutenant Vogel. He phoned me. He didn't know I knew you had an alibi for the Locum kill until I told him. And frankly, from the injuries sustained by those men they picked up at that house, I think you are quite capable of killing."

I shook my head.

"Yes, you are. Maybe not coldly and with premeditation, but both emotionally and physically you sure as hell are equipped for it."

I said nothing.

"You're excused," he said.

"Do you want me to go home, Chief?"

"No. I agree with Sergeant Burns. I don't like the way you work, but you *do* work, and you get results."

"Thank you, sir."

"Drop dead," he said. "Get lost."

That was his dismissal, the copycat. I went back to Helms's office. Vogel was there.

"Did you bring Patty home?" he asked me.

"I did. Want to go with me and question her about Tishkin?"

"Not today. We had to postpone that narcotic bust. Today's the day and we'll need every available man."

I felt as if I was in a time warp.

At the Serano house, Patty was sunning herself in the backyard and Mary was vacuuming the living room, a pleasant domestic scene.

"I didn't think you'd be here until this after-noon," Mary said. "I look a mess!"

"Not to me. Why don't I have a bottle of that Bechtel's Bavarian and watch you vacuum?"

"Chauvinist," she said. "I'll have a bottle with you, and we can talk."

We sat and talked. She said, "You run a small book or sell a little grass, and you figure—who's hurt? Nobody, maybe, but it puts you outside the law, working with people who can hurt, and do. Where do you find true friends then?"

"True friends? You're lucky if you find three in a lifetime, Mary."

"That's what I've finally learned. Family you can trust. These so-called friends we'll talk with today, they've never been that. Locum scares them, but not me. I never paid off to anybody."

"Locum is dead," I said. "He was pushed off a cliff last night."

"Good! I hope he lived long enough to hurt for a while."

My spiritual sister. I said, "You don't know who the collector was before Locum?"

She shook her head. "I never paid."

"I think I know who he is," I said. "I think he was working with Locum and I think he killed Mrs. Marner."

"Why?"

"Because Gonzales and Mrs. Marner were work-ing together to get evidence against him. Jesus probably moved too soon. I think he's dead, just like Maude."

"Are you hungry?" she asked me. "Would you like some lunch?"

"No, thanks. I had a late breakfast."

"So did we," she said. "I'll get cleaned up and we'll visit my former friends."

I headed for my car when we went out, but she said, "Let's take mine. It's air-conditioned."

Through the squalid district the elegant car moved, stopping here, stopping there. I've forgotten most of their faces now and all of their names, except for Leeds. Mary made a point of introducing me to all of them in a clear voice. I didn't realize why until later.

We had finished at the Padilla Grog Shop, and Leeds, too, confirmed my suspicion. But there was no way, he assured us, he would ever repeat it in court.

"You may never have to," Mary told him. "Thanks, Barney. I'll give you my list of customers, if you want them. I'm quitting the business. I'm going to Europe next week with Patty."

"Wonderful!" he said. "Drop me a card, won't you?"

She smiled. "Of course. And I'll make out a list of customers for you."

Outside, she said, "That'll be the day I give him any list." She patted the big black leather purse she'd been carrying. "It's all right here, the first time in history Barney Leeds ever admitted anything to anybody."

"What do you mean?"

"Let's get into the car," she said. "It's hot."

She climbed in behind the wheel and put the purse in my lap. "See that ornamental catch? That hides the microphone and the recording button. Everybody we talked to is in that purse, on tape." She swung the big car away from the curb.

"It's kind of sad, Mary, ending your career as an informer."

"A traitor to my heritage," she admitted. "But for a good cause. I thought an awful lot of Mrs. Marner."

"I don't think this would be admissible in court."

"It's a record for me. I'll bet the police would like to have a copy. And you found out what you wanted to know, didn't you?"

"I did. You're going whole hog, aren't you?"

"I've got my Patty. To hell with all of them. Any of them bother my Patty, I'll have that to hand the police. Maybe it won't convict anybody, but it would sure give the police an excuse to harass them."

At her house, she said, "Come in and have another beer and some spaghetti. And I'll give you your check."

"I'll have the beer and the spaghetti. If you insist on making out a check, make it out for what you think my time was worth and mail it to the Boys' Club downtown."

Too many calories later, she told me at the door, "I'll make a couple extra copies of those tapes for you. You can decide if the police should have one, or part of one. And I'm going to send you a real nice present from Europe."

When I got home, Jan was out in front, hitting cotton golf balls with my old three wood.

"You look owly," she said. "Did something bad happen?"

"Not yet."

"Lieutenant Vogel called. He's going to call again after dinner. He said he'll be busy until then."

"And I'm going to be busy tonight."

"You're tense," she said. "What kind of business is it?"

"I'm going to see a man. I don't want to talk about it. If Vogel's willing, I'd like to take him along."

"Why shouldn't he be willing?"

"It's—too complicated to explain. It's mostly hunch. Let me say, this town is—dirtier than it looks."

24

TWO PEOPLE WERE NOW DEAD, and probably a third, if my hunch on Gonzales was correct. Locum could be a victim of Maude's killer. Or he could have died because he had become powerful enough to attract the attention of some local retirees.

These men had made their fortunes out of co-ordinating the take from all our vices into one giant and efficient network. They knew how easily and completely a city can be destroyed by organized corruption. They didn't want that to happen here, in their peaceful years.

If Locum had been one of their victims, his death would get minimum investigation. As Vill-wock had said, the police had more work than they could handle trying to protect the decent citizens. The murderer of Otis Locum had done both the police and the taxpayers a favor.

When the phone rang, I thought it would be Vogel. But it was Paul Pontius. "I just realized," he said, "that I promised to phone you back last night. But after I phoned Harris and learned you would be released, I saw no reason for it. Apparently you were released."

"I was. And thanks for—calling the right man."

"It has been my experience that going directly to the top man is the best way to get results."

Let's hope he's the top man, I thought. "Thanks again," I said.

"Have they learned anything downtown about that Locum killing?"

"Nothing I know of. But I was only there for half an hour this morning."

"And no suspects in Maude's death?"

"None," I lied.

"Well, hang in there, Brock."

"I intend to," I assured him.

At seven-thirty I phoned Vogel, but there was no answer. I would have to go it alone. Maybe, knowing as little as I did about the alliances in this town, that would be the wiser move, anyway.

It was still light out when I came along the entrance road to the freeway. Traffic was heavy, tourists coming to town for Fiesta Week, for a look at yesterday tomorrow. I took the Avalon turnoff and followed it to Chapparal Road. I turned off that on Ellis Lane.

A goat path, Jerry Jones had called it, and he was right. But once I squeezed around a sharp outcropping of rock, the slope was more gentle, and the view was almost up to Villwock's.

A broad, low house of lightly stained yellow barn siding was at the top of the slope. There was a brand-new pale green camper parked under a metal carport at the side of the house, and an older Plymouth two-door sedan parked on the crushed rock of the parking area next to it.

The man who worshiped in the temple of Mammon had built himself a nice spread.

The porch was as wide as the house. There was no bell; I knocked. The door opened. The smell and sizzle of frying pork drifted out past the wide body of Joe Helms.

"Callahan! What gives?"

"I've learned some more about Tishkin's story. Another lie."

"Come in. I've got some chops frying. Get yourself a beer out of the fridge and sit down."

The living room was immense, with open rafters. The kitchen and eating area had a lower ceiling. I didn't get a beer. I sat in one of the chairs near the dining table.

The phone rang. "Watch those chops, will you," he asked.

The phone was in the living room, but I could hear him clearly. "I didn't get the chemical toilet, and we don't need it. You can crap through that hole in the floor where the toilet's supposed to go. We'll put a pail under it. Now, stop fretting! I've got a dinner burning on the stove!" He hung up.

He walked past me to the stove and turned off the flame. "Villwock," he explained. "We're going fishing this weekend."

I made no comment.

He was taking a pan of French fries out of the oven when he asked, "What's this about Tishkin?"

"He claimed he saw Gonzales leave town at eight o'clock. That same night, at ten o'clock, two witnesses saw Gonzales in town."

"Where?"

"Walking up this way, up Chapparal Road."

"Maybe they did and maybe they didn't. I guess we've both dealt with a lot of unreliable witnesses."

He put his plate of chops and fries on the table without looking at me. He sat down, picked up a fork and finally looked at me. "You didn't come all the way up here to tell me Lenny Tishkin is a liar. What's bugging you?"

"A theory. I have this pattern, and I'd like your professional reaction to it."

"Shoot," he said, and started to eat.

"Si Marner told me his mother was shopping around for a private investigator. Now, why would she do that?"

"Who knows?" he continued to eat.

"She must have known every cop on the force. If she had something that needed investigating, why didn't she go to one of them?"

"You tell me."

"It just hit me a couple days ago. She must have been investigating cops, she and Gonzales together. And then I remembered something your neighbor up the road told me."

I had his attention now. He stopped eating and looked up. "You mean Villwock?"

"Villwock. Maude used to go up there and talk over her problems with him. But two days before she died, though, he noticed she was troubled, she wouldn't confide in him."

"And you're reading that to mean she was investigating cops, and she didn't trust Villwock to go along with it?"

"Maybe not cops. Maybe *one* cop, a cop who might be a friend of Villwock's."

He glared at me, his face rigid. "You're walking on real thin ice, Callahan. Why come here? Why didn't you take this story to the chief?"

I said, "He's a cop, too."

"Easy, now—you're getting close to a punch in the nose. Don't let your size give you any ideas. I've knocked over bigger men."

"Cool it, Sergeant. This isn't anything a prosecutor could take into court. Bear me out."

"Go on."

"Tishkin changed his story when he came back from Morro Bay. How would he know, way up there in Morro Bay, that Nowicki had invalidated his first story? How would he know he needed a new one?''

''Because I questioned him about his first story up there.''

''I see. Well, that makes sense.''

''You got some angles that don't?''

''At least one. That day I walked into your office and you had just finished talking to Mary Serano on the phone.''

A quick interest in his eyes. I had hit a nerve.

''Mary told me later she had already given you all the information you needed on the phone. Why drag me out there to hear it all over again?''

''I'm dying to hear your theory on that.''

''Because it suddenly occurred to you that the hoodlum could serve as a red herring. He could lead me down the road to Mafia involvement. And that was a dead-end road—on this murder.''

''Peeper, you've come up with a lot of dumb theories, but no hard facts.''

''That's true enough, so far. The way I've heard it, around town, Locum is the man they pay, the collector. But who was behind Locum, who was the previous collector? It could be the man who knew this out of town muscle, who tried to force Mary into paying.''

''Why don't you fly to Vegas and ask him?''

I said, ''His name is Francis Martin. Know him?''

His hand jerked, resting on the table. In the heavy silence I thought I heard the scrape of a shoe outside. Helms shook his head.

''He used to call himself Frank Martino,'' I said.

''Never heard of him.''

''You went to high school with him.''

His voice was hoarse and deadly. ''You've got a big nose and a big mouth and a small brain—and no case. When you get a case, take it to the chief."

He stood up abruptly and headed for the living room. He had a gun in there. I had seen it, in its holster, on a table, when I came in. I had no gun.

I stood up and got ready to move. A moving target is harder to hit. I said, "Okay, I'll take it to the chief."

He didn't come back with a gun, only with a package of cigarettes. Again, I thought I heard footsteps outside, this time on the porch. I continued to walk toward the door. I opened it—and saw the shadow of a man.

The man would have to be standing against the wall of the house, between this door and the dim light coming through the living-room window behind him.

Villwock? He could see this house from his place. He could see anyone who came and left. He, too, could be in on the take. He could also be armed.

A moving target was still my safest route and the great outdoors had more places where a man could hide. I was ready to make my run for it. Helms still didn't have a gun in his hand, but he was close enough to reach it now.

He said, "Before you go, peeper, you got anything more solid than those kooky theories?"

"Some testimonies on tape. They are from people who used to pay you off, before you teamed up with Locum. Don't panic; it's nothing I could take into court. But if we combed the acreage up here, there could be a grave. And there might still be traces of carbon monoxide in that camper."

"You son of a bitch!" he growled. "You really mean to nail me, don't you?"

"Only if you're guilty, Joe."

I went out, slamming the door behind me,

crouching low, to avoid a quick shot from the man on the porch, and scrambled down the steps.

I was about twenty feet from the porch when the door opened again. Helms shouted, "Hold it, Callahan! Stay right where you are, if you want to live."

And then another voice. It wasn't Villwock's. It was Vogel's. "Don't do anything foolish, Joe. You're an easy target in that light."

In Captain Dahl's office, Vogel said, "You're really insane! Did you think your size might scare him? Do you really think you're bigger than his .38?"

"The fact speaks for itself. Here I sit, still breathing."

"The thought never occurred to you to take a police officer along?"

"Which one? How could I be sure which one to pick? You, sure. But you didn't phone, and when I phoned you, you weren't home. How come you knew I'd be out there?"

"My wife inherited Maude's long nose. She told me you'd been asking about Frank Martino and had checked the annuals. I don't know the man, but I know the name from some of the locals I play poker with. They seem proud of his big-shot connections."

"That was three days ago, Bernie."

"I know. But tonight we were coming home from a restaurant, and she told me Helms had been a classmate of Martino's. I phoned your house, and your wife told me you had gone out to meet some man. As a matter of fact, I've been leery of Helms myself, lately."

"Sure. When the hell is Harris going to get here? I want to go home."

"Sit tight. I'll get you a cup of coffee."

Dahl came in while he was gone. I said, "I don't suppose you'll be digging around Helms's place in the dark?"

"There's no hurry. He knows we will, so he's already cooked up a story. He said Gonzales came up and threatened him, came with a gun."

"Not that one! They struggled—and the gun went off?"

Dahl nodded. "Joe's not very imaginative. On Mrs. Marner's death he's got an even phonier story. She came up there and had a heart attack. But we've got the hose he used, and it still stinks of carbon monoxide. I suppose he ran it through that hole where the chemical toilet is supposed to be connected."

"I suppose."

Dahl shook his head. "You know what? Helms was the leading contender for this year's Good Samaritan medal!"

Vogel came in with my coffee. "The chief is here. He wants to talk with you in his office. You can take the coffee along."

Chief Chandler Harris was behind his desk, wearing his Santa Claus mask. "Sit down, Mr. Callahan."

I did as directed.

"First of all," he said, "I must thank you. You are a very foolish man, sir, but also very brave."

I smiled modestly.

"Also," he said, "you quite often speak out without measuring the effect of your words."

I'll get a ruler, I thought. "I guess," I said.

"This case," he went on, "has drawn a lot of attention. There are a number of reporters waiting in the assembly room. Not only from this area, but stringers from some of the big city papers."

"I won't need to be there, will I? I want to go home."

"You won't need to be there. I intend to play down Helms's participation in this case. You can understand that, can't you?"

"Of course. Anything new on Locum? Do you think that could have been Helms's work, too?"

He shook his head. "He was giving a talk to some City College students when Locum was killed."

"How about Pontius? Do you think he knows who killed Locum?"

"Why should he?"

"Just a dumb theory of mine. Sorry I mentioned it."

His face was sterner. "You don't have a very high regard for me, do you?"

"I'm sure it's higher than your regard for me, sir. I wouldn't want your job. I know I couldn't handle it."

"Now about those tapes you mentioned," he said. "You'll give us a copy, won't you?"

"Nope."

"And why not?"

"They're not admissible in court, but they could be a source for harassment for the people I talked with. And those are my people, Chief, penny-ante bookies and free-lance hookers. Losers are my people. I fight tigers, not lambs."

"You're a strange man."

"I guess. Well, I came into this case through the front door, but I'll go out through the back. I won't embarrass you."

"Damn you! Do you think I'm a crook?"

"No way, sir. You're doing the best you can in an impossible job. I'm on your side, believe me."

I went out through the back door and into the dark night. So, I had done some good. Don and

Dianne were back in Mill Valley, Patty was with her mother. As any good quarterback will tell you, you can only take what the opposition will give you. They had given me that.

I would go home to my Jan and we would drink cocoa in our snug little house, while the wolves prowled the dark night.

Be a detective.
See if you can solve . . .

Raven House
MINUTE
MYSTERY #3

On the following page is Raven House
MINUTE MYSTERY #3, "Alibi."

Every month each Raven House book will feature a
MINUTE MYSTERY, a unique little puzzler designed
to let *you* do the sleuthing!

U.S. (except Arizona) residents may check their
answer by calling **1-800-528-1404** during the
months of January and February 1982. U.S. residents
may also obtain the solution by writing anytime
during or after this period to:

> Raven House MINUTE MYSTERY
> 1440 South Priest Drive
> Tempe, AZ 85281

Canadian residents, please write to the following
address:

> Raven House MINUTE MYSTERY
> 649 Ontario Street
> Stratford, Ontario N5A 6W2

ALIBI

The professor was in an expansive mood.

"I've often observed," he told his dinner guests, "how extremely difficult it is to fake an unassisted alibi. The recent Werner affair in Chicago is a case in point."

He fired a cigar and continued. "I had no suspicion of Werner when I bumped into him on Michigan Avenue the morning after a friend of his had been found murdered. When I casually inquired where he'd been between four and six o'clock the previous afternoon, he gave the following account.

"'It was such a glorious afternoon that about two o'clock I went for a sail. When I was about eight miles offshore—about 5:30—the wind died down completely. There wasn't a breath of air. Drifting about I recalled that the international distress signal is a flag flown upside down, so I ran mine to the top of the mast in that manner and waited in the dead calm.

"'Shortly after six o'clock the freighter, *Luella*, heaved to, and I went aboard her after securing my boat with a towline. Her skipper said he'd seen my distress signal about three miles away. He put me ashore at Harvey's Landing, and a passing car gave me a lift to town. Imagine my surprise when I read in the morning paper that the *Luella* had sunk in a storm last night and all hands had been lost!'"

The professor sipped his wine and went on. "While the *Luella* had been sunk with loss of entire crew, I immediately arrested Werner for further questioning. I knew his alibi was faked."

How did the professor know?